DR. MORELLE INVESTIGATES

When Brian Cartwright receives a death threat, he calls in the famous criminologist Dr. Morelle to protect him. Apparently, he is to die at 9 p.m. that same day. So with Cartwright alone, locked inside his study — windows and doors sealed — Dr. Morelle waits in an adjoining room, also locked . . . Yet when Dr. Morelle re-enters the study afterwards, he finds Cartwright's body slumped on his desk, shot neatly through the head — and not by his own hand!

ERNEST DUDLEY

DR. MORELLE INVESTIGATES

Complete and Unabridged

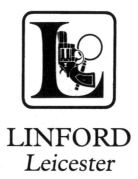

LINFORD
Leicester

First published in Great Britain

First Linford Edition
published 2010

British Library CIP Data

Dudley, Ernest.
  Dr. Morelle investigates. - -
(Linford mystery library)
1. Morelle, Doctor (Fictitious character)- -
Fiction. 2. Criminologists- -Fiction.
3. Death threats- -Fiction. 4. Murder- -
Investigation- -Fiction. 5. Detective and
mystery stories. 6. Large type books.
I. Title II. Series
823.9'14–dc22

ISBN 978-1-44480-186-6

Published by
F. A. Thorpe (Publishing)
Anstey, Leicestershire

Set by Words & Graphics Ltd.
Anstey, Leicestershire
Printed and bound in Great Britain by
T. J. International Ltd., Padstow, Cornwall

LOCKED ROOM MURDER

(Adapted from the stage play
'Doctor Morelle'
by Ernest Dudley and Arthur Watkyn)

1

Brian Cartwright sat working at his desk in his Chelsea house. It was 11.45 p.m. and a Saturday night. Cartwright was a man in his mid-fifties, smooth and polished. The furnishings in the room reflected his impeccable taste.

Behind him, the curtains were drawn across the French windows that led to his large garden. To the front and side of his desk was a large, expensively brocaded sofa, a small mahogany table beside it, from which a radio was playing music. A drinks cabinet stood against one wall, and a standard lamp and several padded chairs completed the furniture in the room. On the mantel above the fireplace reposed an ornate antique clock.

Cartwright glanced up at the sound of a telephone ringing in the hall, the door to which was ajar.

'It's probably them, Miles,' he called through the open door. 'I'll take it in here

— switch it through to me, will you?'

Seconds later the phone on his desk rang, and he picked up the receiver.

'Hello . . . ? Oh, it's you, Stewart! Thought it might have been some friends I'm expecting . . . You spoke to Dawsons? What did they say . . . ? By Wednesday next . . . That's their last word?' Cartwright reflected for a moment, tightening his lips. Then:

'Well, you've done all you can and I'm grateful. I don't know what I'm going to do, but I'll have to think of something . . . Good night.'

He put down the receiver thoughtfully, and looked at his watch. Then he opened a drawer on his desk and took out a revolver, fingering it pensively. He slowly raised it, taking aim in the direction of the hall door.

As he did so, his manservant came in with a decanter and glasses on a tray. He gave a violent start and almost dropped the tray.

'I wish you wouldn't do that, sir. It might be loaded.'

Cartwright smiled pleasantly. 'It is, Miles.'

4

Miles set the tray down on the drinks table as Cartwright returned the revolver to his desk.

'Oh, Miles, that young man who called this afternoon . . . Mr. er — ?'

'Guthrie, sir.'

Cartwright nodded. 'Guthrie. He's a journalist; he's writing some articles on 'Criminal corners of London'. This house is apparently one of them.'

The manservant raised an eyebrow, 'I beg your pardon, sir?'

Cartwright smiled faintly. 'Some female was battered to death a hundred years ago where your pantry is now. He wants to have a look round, take some photographs.' He shrugged carelessly. 'I said he could come Monday or Tuesday night.' He rose from the desk as Miles looked at him enquiringly.

'I'm almost certain to forget. If I'm out when he calls, let him in.'

'I will, sir.' Miles paused, and added hesitantly: 'It's — a quarter to twelve.' He stood aside as Cartwright crossed to the drinks table and began mixing a drink.

'Thank you, Miles.'

'They should be here, sir.' There was an edge of reproach in the manservant's usually respectful voice.

'They should have been here five hours ago,' Cartwright agreed, tilting his drink.

'You don't appear very worried.'

'Have you ever seen me worried, Miles?'

'No, sir.'

'Then go to bed.'

'Yes, sir.' Miles crossed slowly to the door while Cartwright finished his drink and put down his glass. Miles turned. 'It's the car. I do wish you hadn't let them have it.'

'My dear Miles, when friends pile up their own machine on your doorstep and their whole day's gone west without one . . .'

'I suppose you *had* to lend it. But what people can do once, they can do again. And,' Miles added unhappily, 'they seemed in such very high spirits when they left!'

Cartwright smiled. 'You're getting like one of those servants, Miles, who regards his employer's possessions as his own.'

'I take a pride in the car, sir. I shan't be happy until it's back.'

'And in your imagination my friends are already reposing in a ditch beneath it,' Cartwright said sardonically.

'I didn't say so.'

'But you thought it!'

'Yes, sir.'

Cartwright turned back to his desk. 'Go to bed. You shall hear the worst in the morning.' Still the manservant hovered in the doorway, as Cartwright settled again at his desk. 'Have you locked up?'

'Not the dining room windows.'

'Then you'd better do them before you go.'

'Yes, sir.' Miles came back into the room and crossed to the door on the other side of the room.

'Is Mr. Smith in?' Cartwright asked abruptly.

'Not yet, sir.'

As Miles reached the dining room door there came a prolonged ring from the front door bell. He turned and looked at the smiling Cartwright.

'You may not only go to bed, Miles,

you may go to sleep . . . ' As Miles crossed hurriedly to the hall door, Cartwright added dryly: ' . . . Unless, of course, it's the ambulance.'

Miles half turned and looked at him reproachfully before going out.

Cartwright rose and crossed to the table beside the sofa. As he turned the radio down to a minimum, confused and excited voices could be heard coming from the hall.

Cartwright picked out muttered apologies about the time and references to someone named Nigel. After a moment a man appeared at the door. He was a little unsteady on his feet, and put out a hand to the doorframe before advancing into the room.

'Hello, Brian.'

'Hello, Philip.'

Philip Troon was an ex-military type in his early forties. Cartwright regarded him amusedly.

'Little late, I'm afraid.'

'Think nothing of it,' Cartwright shrugged.

Troon glanced back over his shoulder towards the hall. 'Where the devil's Nigel?

Nigel!' He turned to Cartwright. 'Confounded nuisance chaps who don't stick with everyone else. At this time of night, too. Don't you agree, Brian?'

'Definitely.'

Troon made his way unsteadily to a chair by the desk and sat down. 'It's been quite a party, old chap. You know how these things start: we had lunch at Hindhead, went on to the races . . . '

'All right, Philip, I understand,' Cartwright said amiably.

'Knew you would. Told the others that. Said 'Let's get along to old Brian, he'll understand. He'll understand *everything*'.'

'Everything?' Cartwright repeated sharply.

But Troon was looking back distractedly at the hall entrance. 'Can't think where the devil Nigel . . . ' He broke off as a woman entered the room from the hall.

June Lister was a hard-boiled sophisticate, and looked entirely self-possessed as she came forward. Blessed with extraordinary good looks, she had enjoyed a modestly successful career in show business.

'I wouldn't worry about Nigel,' she

9

said. 'He's asleep.'

'Where?' Cartwright was beginning to sense that something was not quite right.

'In the car,' she explained. 'Hello, Brian.' She crossed to the fireplace.

'Where's Evelyn?' Cartwright asked.

'Powdering her nose.' June was looking critically into the mirror above the mantelpiece, 'God, I look awful.'

'Impossible, my dear,' Cartwright smiled.

With an effort, Troon pulled himself together. 'Didn't I tell you, June, old Brian would understand?'

'There's nothing *to* understand,' June said sharply. She glanced at Cartwright. 'We had a little party. That's all. Ten thousand apologies, Brian, for keeping the car out so late.' She seated herself at the end of the sofa.

'Last race of the day, old boy, tote double,' Troon said vaguely. 'Easy come, easy go.'

'We had dinner in Guildford. You know how time flies,' June said.

'There's no need to explain,' Cartwright said, moving around to the side of his desk.

'That's right.' Troon said quickly. 'No need to explain. Just get ourselves home, that's the thing, and the old car's fine. Not a scratch . . . '

'Philip . . . ' June frowned at him.

'Is the car all right?' Cartwright asked levelly.

June rose and crossed to the fireplace again. 'Yes, Brian, of course . . . the car's all right.'

There was an awkward silence, then they all turned to look at the hall entrance as a young woman came in.

She was perhaps ten years younger than the other woman, and decidedly less worldly. She appeared nervous, highly strung, and looked as if she was on the verge of tears.

'Philip, I — I feel so shivery. Hello, Brian.'

Troon rose and went over to her. 'My darling,' he said protectively.

'It's a horrid feeling, isn't it?' she shuddered, as he put an arm about her shoulders.

'Have a drink?' Cartwright suggested, seeking to ease the tension in the room.

Evelyn seated herself gingerly on the sofa. 'No, thank you.'

'It'll do you good,' Cartwright encouraged.

'No, no. I never want to see a drink again.' She looked up at Troon. 'Do you hear me? Never!'

Troon attempted to smile reassuringly. 'Evelyn, darling — '

'What's so funny about that?' Evelyn's voice rose shrilly.

'Nothing funny, only . . . we all go through that stage.' Troon was becoming vague again. 'I remember swearing off the stuff for life. Went to bed and dreamed of rows and rows of bottles of lemonade.'

'It's time we all went home,' June interposed deliberately. 'Philip, go and get Nigel out of the car, so that Brian can put it away.'

As Troon moved towards the door, Evelyn rose quickly. 'He can't put it away!' she blurted out. 'No one can put the car away.'

'Eve — ' Troon said awkwardly.

'Why not?' Cartwright asked deliberately, sensing that the explanation of his guest's odd behaviour was about to come out.

'We've got to look at it first,' Evelyn said firmly.

'Evelyn . . . ' Troon returned to the end of the sofa, his brow furrowed. He eased Evelyn back onto the sofa.

'What's wrong with the car?' Cartwright pursued.

'Nothing,' June shrugged carelessly. 'She doesn't know what she's talking about.'

Evelyn flushed. 'I do know what I'm talking about. You've got to look at it, Brian. All over.'

'Why?' Cartwright was genuinely puzzled.

'Because — because we hit something,' Evelyn said brokenly,

'For God's sake!' Troon exclaimed.

'Did you?' Cartwright demanded.

'No, of course we didn't,' June cut in dismissively. 'She's got a fixed idea something hit the car just after we left Esher.'

Evelyn got up again. 'You know we hit something.'

'May have been the branch of a tree or a bird against the windscreen,' Troon suggested,

13

'It wasn't that.' Evelyn persisted.

'We had a good look when we got here,' June said calmly.

'Not a scratch to show,' Troon added.

'There didn't have to be,' Evelyn objected.

'If you hit something there would be,' Cartwright said, frowning.

Evelyn sat down again on the end of the sofa, her lips trembling. 'It wasn't just 'something'. It was a man and we killed him.'

There was total silence for a moment.

June seated herself beside the distraught younger woman. 'Brian, she's in a state where she hasn't the least idea what she's saying.'

Cartwright ignored her at looked sharply at Evelyn. 'How d'you know it was a man?'

'I saw him. We all saw him. I told them to stop.'

'Did they?' Cartwright asked sharply.

'No,' Evelyn whispered.

Cartwright looked at the others. 'Why not?'

'They said it was best to drive on,'

Evelyn said quietly.

'Is that true?' Cartwright aimed a glance at June. She rose and walked to the fireplace, then turned.

'Yes, Brian.'

'My God,' Troon said agitatedly, 'why do we have to go into all this now? The thing's done and finished with.'

'Who was driving?' Cartwright pursued. None of the others answered him. Instead, they were all looking at the hall doorway. Cartwright swung to follow their gaze.

In the hall doorway had appeared the drunken figure of Nigel Forbes. He swayed for a moment, then lurched forward and flopped into the nearest chair.

'That's why we drove on,' June said dryly.

Evelyn rose restlessly. 'We could have done something . . . got him to hospital. We just left him in the road . . . '

June glared at Troon. 'If you can't control your girlfriend . . . ' she began.

Cartwright had resumed his seat at his desk, and regarded the others. 'I'm at least indebted to her for the truth,' he said.

'How do we know it's the truth?' June snapped. 'There's no proof we hit anyone. We all saw a man, he was close to the car — there was a sort of bump . . . '

'Which could have been something on the road,' Troon put in. 'And we were several hundred yards away before we knew what had happened.'

Troon crossed where Cartwright sat at his desk before continuing: 'We were doing seventy. If we hit him, old chap, there's nothing we could have done.'

'It might have been polite to inquire,' Cartwright said acidly.

'And what sort of mess would we have been in?' June remained unrepentant. 'Nigel was tight, Brian — ' She pointed at him, ' — as tight as that! And not for the first time with a car.'

Troon looked at Cartwright appealingly. 'He'd have gone to prison.' He paused, then added: 'We'd all have been in it. Headlines, front-page stuff.'

'I wouldn't mind about myself,' June observed.

Troon shook his head irritably. 'You can't talk like that. He glanced at Cartwright. 'Her new show, Brian, opening next week; her first big break, perhaps the start of everything.'

Evelyn began pacing the room. 'What do any of us matter?'

'Don't you even care about Philip?' June asked sharply.

Troon spread his hands. 'She doesn't understand — '

'Well, it's time she did,' June snapped. She glared at Evelyn. 'Every penny he's got has been sunk in that precious hotel he's bought for you to run. If this came out, not a soul would come near the place. You'd crash in a week. Does that register?'

Evelyn did not answer. Instead she gripped Troon's arm. 'Philip, please take me home.'

'I think that would be a wise move,' Cartwright commented.

'Well, aren't you going to say something else, Brian?' June demanded. Aren't you going to tell her we did the only possible thing?'

'I'm sorry,' Cartwright apologised. He looked at Evelyn. 'They did the only possible thing, my dear,' he said dryly.

'It was a filthy, rotten thing,' Evelyn said heatedly, 'and I hope I never wake up to remember it.'

'Come along, darling, please.' Holding her arm, Troon started to take Evelyn to the door. Suddenly she pulled away from him and hurried to the door herself, and out into the hall.

Troon moved to follow her, then paused to shake Forbes by the shoulder.

'Nigel! We're going home!' As Forbes rose unsteadily to his feet he added: 'We'll get a taxi.'

He went out after Evelyn, Forbes stumbling along behind.

June moved over to the desk and looked at Cartwright steadily. 'It's hardly necessary to mention that what we've told you is in confidence.'

Cartwright smiled thinly. 'I rather gathered that.'

'We regard you as a friend.'

'I appreciate the compliment.'

Troon reappeared in the hall doorway,

'Can we drop you, June?'

'No, thanks, it isn't far. I'll walk . . . Good night, Brian. Good night, Philip.'

She went out past Troon. He closed the door and turned to look back at Cartwright.

At that moment, the faint sound of the music on the radio, which had remained on as background noise during their conversation, came to an end.

'Sorry, old chap, about all this,' Troon said.

'I'm sorry for you,' Cartwright said, getting up and moving to the drinks table where he picked up his glass and poured out a drink. Idly, he listened to the radio as an announcer's voice sounded faintly.

'Don't think you really need be,' Troon said, coming back into the room and leaning against the mantelpiece. 'After all, we don't know exactly what happened. Chap can make a mistake in the dark; especially when it's been a bit of an evening . . . ' He paused, and the voice of an announcer on the radio became faintly audible.

'This is the B.B.C. Light Programme. Before the late news summary here is an announcement. The London Electricity Board announce that on Tuesday next there will be a change over in the South Western Area to a new grid system . . . '

'Must be twelve o'clock,' Troon remarked.

Cartwright pointed at the clock on the mantelpiece and crossed to the radio. 'Four minutes to.'

The voice of the radio announcer came again: ' . . . During the switchover the electric current may be turned off for a moment. The time for the changeover will be given later.'

'Afraid I've rather lost track of the time,' Troon said vaguely. 'One does, you know.'

'Of course,' Cartwright agreed,

'What about the car?' Troon asked.

'I'll put it away,' Cartwright assured him.

'Well . . . I'll be getting along. Good night, old man.'

As Cartwright again moved to the door, Cartwright turned the radio up.

' . . . on the Kingston bypass at ten

forty-five tonight. A man was knocked down by a car, proceeding in the direction of London, and received injuries from which he has since died. Will anyone who witnessed the accident, or who has any information regarding it please communicate with New Scotland Yard, telephone . . . '

Troon stood perfectly still as Cartwright switched off the radio.

'Well, that's that,' he said quietly, as Cartwright straightened and faced him directly. 'Poor devil. If we'd known, of course, we'd have gone back.'

'It's a little late for excuses,' Cartwright said levelly.

'The thing's done now and there's nothing more to be said about it,' Troon said thickly. Then, as Cartwright remained silent, he added plaintively: 'Is there, Brian?' He advanced slowly towards Cartwright, as he moved to his desk.

Cartwright turned to look at him. 'A moment ago you observed that a chap can make a mistake in the dark. You made a mistake tonight; a bad one.'

'What do you mean?' Troon demanded

nervously. 'Now let's get this clear. You're going to see us through this. You're going to stand by us.'

'The police are asking for information. It's everyone's duty to cooperate. Failure to do so might be an offence.'

'What the hell!' Troon protested,

'To say nothing of the burden on one's conscience,' Cartwright said implacably. 'You're asking a lot, Philip.'

'But you must see that we can't . . . ' Troon was now thoroughly alarmed.

'I hope you'll be duly appreciative when I say that I'm going to stand by you,' Cartwright said smoothly.

Relief spread over Troon's face.

'Well, why the devil didn't you say so in the first place?' Troon continued awkwardly: 'That makes everything all right, then. And it's hardly necessary, my dear fellow, for me to express . . . '

'It's not necessary.' Cartwright said briefly.

'Only to say — thank you. Thanks a lot, old chap.' Troon hesitated, and turned again to the door. 'And — good night.'

Cartwright spoke quietly from his desk.

'Oh, Philip. Just one small point.'

Troon turned at the door.

'I hope you'll regard it as no more than a coincidence that I have an appointment in the City on Wednesday.'

'In the City?' Troon was puzzled.

'With my brokers,' Cartwright said amiably. 'A little matter of settling an account. They're pressing me, for three thousand pounds.' Troon stared at him, baffled. 'Quite a lot of money, Philip. It would take a great weight off my mind if I could be obliged with a trifling temporary loan. Say, two thousand.'

'Two thousand?' Troon moved slowly back into the room.

'Between the four of you that shouldn't be embarrassing,' Cartwright said.

'Brian!' The meaning of Cartwright's words finally registered on Troon.

Cartwright smiled. 'My dear fellow, if it can't be arranged you've only to say so. I shall quite understand and the deal is off,' he paused and added gently: 'on both sides.'

Troon advanced to the desk where Cartwright sat smiling blandly. 'Just good old-fashioned blackmail. You damned swine!'

'Harsh words, Philip, to one who is only trying to help.' Unfazed, Cartwright opened his diary. 'By the way, to avoid any misunderstanding may we say by nine o'clock on Tuesday night? Failing which, I shall find myself obliged to do my duty as a law-abiding member of the public.'

Troon, his face contorted, moved forward menacingly, only to pull up short as Cartwright reached into his drawer and brought out the revolver.

'Sorry, Philip. But this is one you can't drive past.'

The two men faced each other, and then Troon seemed to sag.

'Good night, Philip,' Cartwright said calmly.

As Troon turned for the hall door, there came a sound as the dining room door clicked open.

'What's that?' Troon said sharply.

'It's all right, Philip,' Cartwright smiled. It's only Mr. Smith. My Siamese cat.'

2

It was 8.30 p.m. on the following Tuesday night. Voices sounded through the open dining room door in the study at the Chelsea home of Brian Cartwright.

Miles entered Cartwright's study and switched on the lights in the room, looked round to make sure room was tidy. After straightening the cushions on the sofa he went out, leaving the door open.

Evelyn stood in the other doorway of the study, having entered from the adjoining dining room. She glanced back over her shoulder. 'No, I'll be quite all right, thank you.'

'Sure?' Troon's voice sounded from the dining room behind her.

'Yes.' With that, Evelyn came in from the dining room and closed the door behind her.

She crossed to the hall door to make sure no one was coming, then returned and put her evening bag down on the arm of the sofa. She went up to the desk, opened a drawer and took out Cartwright's revolver.

As she began to return with the revolver, Miles came back into the room carrying a whiskey decanter on a tray.

Hurriedly, Evelyn held the revolver behind her back. 'Oh, Miles!'

'I'm sorry if I startled you. Mr. Cartwright is always complaining I walk too quietly.'

Evelyn gave a nervous laugh. 'It's — it's a good fault . . . ' She paused as Miles set down the tray on the drinks table, then: 'Miles, what was the idea of this dinner party?'

'The idea? Is there anything unusual in Mr. Cartwright inviting his friends?'

'In this case I think there is.' Evelyn tightened her lips.

'Oh . . . ' Miles smiled and moved to the door. 'I can assure you if you think he was annoyed about the other evening . . . '

'I said nothing about the other evening,' Evelyn said quickly.

Miles was puzzled. 'But you seemed to think it was strange.'

'Please forget what I said.'

'As you wish.' Miles gave her an odd look, then went out.

Evelyn moved to the sofa, picked up her evening bag and put the revolver inside. As she seated herself on the sofa, June came in from the dining room.

'Did you get anything out of Miles, Evelyn?'

'No.'

'He's no idea why we've been asked?'

Evelyn shrugged. 'Just Brian's natural hospitality.'

June crossed to the fireplace. 'Natural, my eye. I'd give a lot to know what his game is.'

'You don't think it may be to — to call the whole thing off? To tell us it was just a joke in bad taste?'

June shook her head. 'That's not Brian's way. But why invite those other two? That's what puzzles me. Complete strangers who've got nothing whatever to do with it.'

'Did you find out who they are?' Evelyn asked.

'I think one of them's a reporter — '

'A *what?*'

'A reporter, dear.'

Evelyn stood up quickly and stared at the older woman. 'You don't suppose Brian's told them?'

'Oh dear, no.' June was certain. 'Brian doesn't throw away good cards like that.'

'Then why's he asked him?'

June smiled grimly. 'A sadistic touch, perhaps; to put the wind up us properly. Charming, isn't it?'

'I can't stand it!' Evelyn's voice rose. 'I can't, June. If he goes through with this, it'll finish Philip. He'll have lost every penny, he'll be completely ruined.' She sank back on to the sofa.

'Pity you didn't think of that the other night,' June admonished.

'I didn't know what I was saying or doing.'

June lit herself a cigarette. 'Which of us did? That's why we're in this mess'.

Evelyn sighed. 'If only we could wake up and find it was all a dream.'

Philip Troon entered from the dining room. 'Evelyn! What's the matter?'

June sat back in an armchair facing the

sofa. 'She wishes the other night was a dream.'

Troon went across to the distraught Evelyn. 'What's the use of talking like that, darling? Don't we all?'

'I'm sorry, Philip.'

'You want to be sorry for anyone, make it Nigel,' Troon said. 'He hasn't closed his eyes since he found out what really happened.'

'Oh, I know.'

'Yes, but keeping awake isn't going to undo it,' Troon said grimly. 'Nor will anything any of us can do now. All we can do is go to the police, and make sure we smash up four other lives as well. Is that what you want us to do?'

'No.'

'Well, then, you've got to control yourself.'

Evelyn nodded miserably, then said: 'Philip, we've got to talk to Brian! We've got to get him alone, away from those other two.'

'I can't think why they're here,' June commented. 'The affair's no business of theirs at all.'

Troon glanced at her. 'I don't know why Brian asked them.'

A new voice sounded: 'Don't you? I'll tell you.'

They all turned as Nigel Forbes entered the room. His face showed the effects of lack of sleep. But his voice was firm, if slightly mechanical as he added: 'They were asked here to stop us talking. So that instead of having the whole thing out with Brian as we want to, we were forced to make polite conversation.'

Evelyn frowned. 'Yes, but . . . '

Forbes moved to the end of the sofa. 'All Brian wants from us tonight is the money he's asked for. And he wants it without argument. By inviting strangers as well he's made sure there won't be any.'

'I think Nigel's right . . . ' June said slowly, then broke off as a young man in a lounge suit came in from the dining room.

'And what's Nigel right about?' the young man asked artlessly.

'My name is Forbes.' Coldly.

'Beg pardon,' the other smiled, producing a cigarette. 'Got a light?'

Forbes grudgingly gave him a light.

Troon snapped, 'Now listen, Mr. — '

'The name is Bill Guthrie.' The young man drew at his cigarette, then crossed to the side of the desk in front of the French windows.

'I'd like to ask you a personal question,' Troon pursued.

'Ask away.'

'Why were you invited here tonight?' Troon asked bluntly.

Guthrie seated himself in a chair to the right of the desk. 'I think it was to have dinner.'

'Apart from that,' Troon snapped.

'The pleasure of talking to you,' Guthrie said blandly.

'Apart from *that?*'

Guthrie smiled faintly. 'Is there any objection to my consulting my lawyers?'

Troon moved restlessly towards the fireplace. 'I mean, was there any special reason?'

Guthrie hesitated. 'Yes — and no.'

Forbes looked up from where he was pouring a drink. 'Make up your mind.'

'Well, you see,' Guthrie explained, 'it's

like this. I'm writing a series of newspaper articles called 'Criminal corners of London'.'

'Is *that* what brought you here?' June was incredulous.

'Sure. This building's on a very historical spot, in a sordid kind of way.'

'What d'you mean?' Evelyn asked.

'One hundred years ago, in eighteen fifty-three, Mary Wright was strangled in the hall. I've figured it was about where Miles's pantry is now.'

'We're not interested in what happened to Mary Wright in the pantry,' June said dismissively.

Guthrie smiled. 'Oh, but I am, intensely. And there's nothing like getting your atmosphere on the spot. So I called on Cartwright on Saturday and asked if I could have a good look round, you know, get the topography right, take some photos. He said, 'Come Monday or Tuesday'. I came Tuesday, and here I am.'

'You found there was a dinner party going on,' June pointed out.

'It hit me in the eye,' Guthrie smiled, 'and I tried to back out. But Cartwright wouldn't let me go. He asked me if I'd be interested in a murder in nineteen fifty-three. I said I was only interested up to the end of the nineteenth century, but when did it happen? He replied, 'It hasn't yet'. I said 'When's it going to?' He said 'Tonight'. I said 'Where?' He said, 'Here', would I care to stay?' He grinned broadly. 'Well, I mean, reporters are only human . . .' He broke off as Cartwright himself entered from the dining room.

'Have you all had coffee?' he asked.

'Look here, Brian,' Troon said curtly, 'what's this cock-and-bull yarn you've been telling Guthrie?'

Cartwright raised an eyebrow, 'Guthrie?'

'About a murder here tonight,' Troon snapped. 'Don't you think it's time you stopped fooling him and sent him home?'

'I have no intention of sending him home,' Cartwright stated quietly.

'Why not?'

'Because I'm not fooling . . . ' he looked towards the door as Miles came in carrying a coffee tray. 'Thank you, Miles. Where's Dr. Morelle?'

June gave a start. 'Dr. Morelle?'

Cartwright glanced at her, 'I felt quite certain I introduced him.'

'I didn't associate the name.'

Cartwright seated himself at his desk. 'Until you heard this cock-and-bull yarn? Oh yes, Dr. Morelle is an expert on — the things Mr. Guthrie writes about.'

Forbes rose from the arm of the sofa where he had been sitting, and went over to the drinks table. 'Another ruddy scribbler!' he muttered.

During these exchanges, Miles had been offering the coffee around. All refused the offer except Cartwright and Guthrie.

'On the contrary,' Guthrie commented, taking a sip, 'Dr. Morelle is an eminent psychiatrist.'

'He is also an expert on crime,' Cartwright added.

'Is that why he's here?' Evelyn asked.

'It is,' Cartwright assented.

Forbes returned to the sofa with his drink. 'Then I'll tell you what's happened to him. It took him about halfway through dinner to sum you up as an irresponsible buffoon and he's done what any sensible man would have done: gone home!'

At that moment a tall, slim and darkly handsome middle-aged man appeared at the French windows leading to the garden. Wearing immaculate evening dress, he entered the room, smiling sardonically.

'Not yet, Mr. Forbes. I have been admiring the view of Battersea power station across the river.'

'Dr. Morelle!' Evelyn exclaimed.

Troon frowned angrily. 'You mean you've been eavesdropping on every word we've said!'

'You suffer from the illusion most people share, that their conversation is worth overhearing,' Dr. Morelle replied calmly.

Troon tightened his lips and sat on an arm of the sofa.

As Miles gave coffees to Dr. Morelle and Cartwright, June Lister spoke sharply: 'I suffer from the old-fashioned idea that it's private. Doctor, if it isn't rude of me, why exactly are you here?'

Dr. Morelle waited until Miles crossed to the door and went out before replying.

'I have been invited to investigate a murder,' he said, moving to take up a position on the right of Cartwright's desk.

June shrugged. 'Well, it happened in the lounge and you're a hundred years too late.'

Cartwright glanced at his watch. 'On the contrary, Dr. Morelle is twenty-eight minutes too soon.'

'You don't say!' June said sarcastically, rising to her feet. 'Well, I don't think I'll stay and witness it. I must get some sleep. I've got an early rehearsal.'

As she moved towards door leading to the hall, Guthrie crossed up to her. 'Rehearsal! You're not *the* June Lister, are you?'

June halted and looked at him. 'I am. Why?'

Guthrie smiled. 'We're giving you a break tomorrow. Half a column on the gossip page. Friend of mine saw you rehearse; he's going to town over you. I've seen the lay out: 'New star in the November sky'.'

'New star in the November sky,' Cartwright repeated thoughtfully. 'You know, I think that might read rather well.'

'Might!' Guthrie exclaimed. 'It's going to.'

'Unless,' Cartwright said gently, 'it were displaced by another item. That, I believe, could happen.' He addressed his next remark directly to June who was again turning to go, 'If you were going out that way, June, the front door is locked.'

The actress spun round. 'Locked?'

There was a silence.

Troon jumped to his feet. 'Now look here, Brian, once and for all . . . '

Forbes had risen also, 'What's the game?'

'Yes, why's that door locked?' Troon demanded. 'Why are we here?'

'You're here to explain,' Cartwright said briefly.

'We're to explain!' Evelyn exclaimed. 'Explain what?'

'A little note one of you has sent me,' Cartwright explained, reaching into his inside pocket. 'It's typewritten. I received it this morning, I'll read it; it's quite short.'

He took the note from his pocket.

'Dear Brian: We have till nine o'clock. So have you. R.I.P.'

He returned the note to his pocket. 'Quite amusing.'

Guthrie gave a puzzled frown. 'And what might all that mean?'

'It means,' Cartwright said deliberately, 'that at nine o'clock I shall give certain information to the police and one of these kind persons would prefer that I did not.'

'What information?' Dr. Morelle asked sharply.

'Brian — 'Troon began, apprehensively.

Cartwright regarded him coldly. 'Don't worry, Philip. You have till nine o'clock.'

'What information?' Dr. Morelle repeated.

Cartwright ignored the question. Instead, he said: 'Now the reason I've invited Dr. Morelle . . . '

'Never mind him,' Forbes interjected. 'Are you seriously suggesting one of us wrote that note?'

'You must have,' Cartwright said levelly.

'Now you're being ridiculous,' Forbes sneered.

Cartwright gave him a sharp glance. 'The note mentions nine o'clock. No one

38

but you four knew about nine o'clock.'

There was an uncomfortable pause as Cartwright's guests glanced at one another uneasily. Troon broke the silence. 'Then I suppose one of us must have written it: just as a joke, of course.'

'Yes,' Evelyn said eagerly. 'A joke, that's all.'

'Somebody trying to be funny,' Troon added.

'If anyone had the damned good idea of bumping you off he'd get on with the job,' Forbes remarked sourly.

'Yes,' Troon agreed. 'He'd hardly advertise the fact by writing you a note.'

Dr. Morelle seated himself in the chair to the right of Cartwright's desk. 'In this case I think he might,' he said.

The others all looked at him.

'In this case?' Evelyn repeated.

'Because a note that mentioned nine o'clock would compromise three other persons,' Dr. Morelle explained. 'What is known as widening the area of suspicion: quite sound.'

Cartwright rose to his feet. 'Thank you, Dr. Morelle.'

'Then sort this out, Dr. Morelle,' Forbes said challengingly. 'The four of us here have no particular love for Brian. But he has an exaggerated idea of his own importance if he thinks we'd risk our necks for him.' He turned to the drinks table and poured himself another drink.

'The note says nothing about risking a neck,' Dr. Morelle pointed out. 'Simply R.I.P.'

Cartwright moved around the left hand side of his desk. 'As to my importance at this particular hour, I'd like Dr. Morelle's opinion.' He paused for a moment, then went on: 'Major Troon has recently had the courage to purchase a small hotel. How brave he has been, only he and his accountants know. Success will be deserved: failure, I suspect, disastrous.' He paused again, to indicate Evelyn. 'Miss Wells was my secretary for six months: sufficient grounds, no doubt, for homicidal intent.'

Troon snapped: 'You can leave Evelyn out of it.'

Cartwright looked at him steadily. 'But not, I fear, out of the hotel. As the Major's bride-to-be, she has a vested

40

interest. It would not be extravagant to suggest — she is likely to share its fate.'

'Brian . . . ' June Lister began to protest as Cartwright turned to look at her implacably.

'Miss Lister, as you have gathered, is about to achieve an ambition, a dangerous hour with any woman. In her profession, opportunity is not in the habit of knocking twice.'

'I could kill you, Brian,' June said levelly. With a contemptuous look, she moved over to the nearest armchair and seated herself.

'You may be going to,' Cartwright said dryly.

'And me?' Forbes demanded belligerently, as Cartwright's gaze switched to him.

'And Nigel Forbes, Doctor, the only one I personally admire,' Cartwright said, with a sideways glance to where Dr. Morelle stood. 'Mr. Guthrie may recall he was one of our leading test pilots; a brave man. He unfortunately lost his nerve, and has tried to recover it — ' he glanced meaningfully at the drink in Forbes's hand — 'in the least satisfactory way.'

Forbes tightened his lips. 'You can leave my personal history . . . '

'He is facing a potential cure,' Cartwright said mockingly. 'The bar does not open in any of Her Majesty's prisons.' Deliberately, he poured himself a liqueur and moved back towards his desk.

'None of these unpleasant things need happen, if I choose to be discreet. But at nine o'clock, failing a simple transaction, I shall have no option but to be indiscreet.'

'Are you sure of that, Brian?' Evelyn asked, her voice strangely tense.

'Quite sure.'

Evelyn faced him. 'Nothing will change your mind?'

'Only one thing,' Cartwright said.

'Not even this?' Evelyn took out his revolver from her handbag, and pointed it at him steadily. He gave a start and slowly began to put down his glass, his eyes on the gun.

'Evelyn — ' Troon whispered.

'I know what I'm doing,' Evelyn said tightly. She looked at Cartwright. 'This was a private affair and it's staying that way,'

Dr. Morelle rose smoothly from his seat. 'My dear young woman . . . '

Evelyn swung, covering him with the gun. 'Don't move,' she warned.

'I merely wished to point out that I should not rely on that revolver,' he said suavely.

'It's loaded all right,' Evelyn snapped.

Dr. Morelle smiled thinly. 'It was — before dinner. I fear that my curiosity is not confined to conversations.'

Involuntarily, Evelyn glanced down at the revolver. As she did so, Dr. Morelle moved forward quickly and wrested the weapon from her. Troon had also moved at the same moment, and firmly gripped his struggling fiancée.

Dr. Morelle handed the weapon to Cartwright, who had quickly recovered his composure. 'Thank you, Doctor.'

As he opened the chamber, his expression suddenly changed. He looked up at the calm features of Doctor Morelle.

'It's loaded! I thought you said . . . '

'There are moments when a little deception is justified,' Dr. Morelle replied suavely.

Troon had led the distraught Evelyn back to the sofa. Weakly she sank back down. Troon sat on the arm, holding her shoulders,

Cartwright glanced at Dr. Morelle. 'The diversion may at least persuade you that my guests are serious. Which of them is most in earnest I have invited you to find out.'

He sat at the desk and replaced his revolver in the drawer.

'I have, in fact, reversed the normal procedure. It has always struck me as anomalous that the police and the press are only called in after a crime has been committed. Why not before?'

'The opportunity is too seldom provided,' Dr. Morelle commented.

'I have provided it.'

Forbes moved again to the back of the sofa. 'The man's raving!'

Cartwright ignored him and looked steadily at Dr. Morelle. 'I have assembled for your benefit, half an hour before the

44

event, the suspects, the motives, and the corpse.'

'What are you getting at?' Troon asked, gently disengaging his arm from Evelyn's shoulders.

'Consider, Mr. Guthrie,' Cartwright glanced at him, 'how many times have you been able to write up a murder before it occurred?'

Guthrie moved down to the left hand side of Cartwright's desk, and looked at the seated man. 'Never,' he said firmly.

'As for myself,' Cartwright resumed, 'what corpse before has had the pleasure of stepping into eternity and the front page at the same time?'

Guthrie's eyes gleamed. 'The front page . . . '

'I thought that would bring you to life,' Cartwright said dryly.

Guthrie became animated. 'Romantic eccentric. Knew he was doomed. Died on time.'

'Unlimited feminine sympathy,' Cartwright added.

'Depending on the photo . . . ' Guthrie snapped his fingers. 'Photo! My God! You can't go on the front page without a photo.' He crossed the front of the desk. 'Would you mind?'

'The victim before the crime,' Cartwright nodded. 'Should be unique.'

'Boy, I'll say so . . . Just getting my camera.' Guthrie hurried out of the room heading for the hall.

'This is fantastic, Brian!' Troon protested.

Forbes moved up to the drinks table, 'Utter damned nonsense!'

'Just because someone writes you a schoolboy note, trying to be funny,' June said.

'I am eager and willing to share the joke,' Cartwright looked calmly from one to the other, then rose from his desk chair. 'Which of you wrote the note?' He waited for an answer.

There was silence.

'Come now, Miss Lister, Major Troon. One of you must have,' Doctor Morelle remarked.

There was still no answer.

'Well, Doctor?' Cartwright asked bluntly.

'Mr. Cartwright is justified in his attitude.' Dr. Morelle turned as Guthrie returned, carrying his camera.

'Now, where exactly do you expect to be murdered?' he asked Cartwright.

'Physically or geographically?'

'Geographically.'

'I propose to remain in this room.'

'Yes, but where in the room?' Guthrie asked. 'Don't think me fussy but, you know, readers like the photo to be on the fatal spot.'

'Of course. Where would you suggest? At my desk?'

Guthrie rested his camera next to the radio on the small table beside the sofa. 'Why not? Busy with your papers, making your will.'

Cartwright sat at the desk and picked up a pen. 'Something like that?'

'Fine,' Guthrie agreed,

'Should I smile?' Cartwright asked dryly.

'It might add pathos.' Guthrie looked up. 'Chin slightly up please. Left hand slightly forward.' Guthrie took a photo. 'Okay!' He straightened, then moved to join June on the sofa.

Cartwright smiled. 'I sincerely trust it will be wasted.'

'There's one good reason why it will be,' Dr. Morelle commented.

'What's that?'

Dr. Morelle moved to the right of the desk where Cartwright still sat. 'The thoroughness of your precautions precludes any possibility of the crime.'

Cartwright was still smiling. 'That, frankly, was the idea.'

'Then,' Dr, Morelle said brusquely, 'you will permit me to take my leave. I have better employment than waiting for something that cannot possibly happen.' He made a move towards the hall door.

'You must remain till nine o'clock,' Cartwright said quietly.

Dr. Morelle turned, 'But, my dear Cartwright . . . '

'When a man is surrounded by enemies, Doctor, anything is possible.' Cartwright smiled disarmingly at the others. 'There are drinks through in the lounge.'

Troon rose quickly. 'That's the first sane thing you've said. Come, Evelyn.' Then, turning to Cartwright he added: 'As for nine o'clock; you may as well know now,

Brian, that my answer will be 'no' and you can go to the police. Is that clear?'

'Quite clear.'

'But, Philip . . . ' Evelyn caught at his arm.

Troon ignored her imprecation and went on his way through the dining room door. Evelyn hesitated only a moment, and then hurried after him. Forbes followed close behind.

At the doorway Forbes turned to Dr. Morelle. 'In case you're wondering what all that meant, our host is expecting us to pay him two thousand pounds or else. I thought you might like to know that your client is a blackmailer.'

Guthrie stood up, 'Is that true?' he asked Cartwright.

June rose alongside him and smiled cynically. 'Shocked, Mr. Guthrie? It's Brian's fault. He's gone to the trouble of introducing the suspects, but forgotten the corpse.'

'I left that for you,' Cartwright said dryly. 'Go ahead.'

'Name: Brian Swinley Cartwright; married twice, no children; lived in South

America, where his business activities covered a multitude of sins. The profits brought him home a year ago. Makes friends easily, too easily. Three nights ago we came to him in a jam. He was kind and sympathetic. So sympathetic he promised to keep his mouth shut — for the sum mentioned, a sum we suspect to be the first of many. Altogether, he's very nice to know.'

'Thank you, my dear,' Cartwright said sarcastically.

June hesitated in the doorway and looked back. 'There's only one thing more. Nigel said just now that whatever you are you're not worth swinging for. Speaking for myself, I wonder.' Without a further backward glance, she followed Troon and the others.

'How brightly doth the old flame burn,' Cartwright mused aloud.

'You mean — you and she — ?' Guthrie said, surprised.

'Oh, yes. Yes, indeed.'

'What happened?' Guthrie asked curiously.

Cartwright sighed, and rose from his seat. 'They say that in all great loves one

tires before the other. A drink, Doctor?'
He crossed to the drinks table.

'After what I have just learned, I'm afraid I can take no further interest in your case,' Dr. Morelle replied curtly.

'If I were already dead, Dr. Morelle, would you have taken no interest then?'

'But you're not going to die,' Guthrie protested. 'Talk sense, man. How?'

'How?' Cartwright murmured. 'You enjoyed your coffee?'

'My coffee?' Guthrie frowned. 'Yes — '

Cartwright glanced at Dr. Morelle. 'And you?'

Dr. Morelle nodded.

'Good.'

'You mean,' Guthrie faltered, 'it may have been drugged?'

'You asked me how? For all I know I'm already dying, scheduled by the laws of chemistry to expire at nine o'clock.'

'You — you shouldn't have drunk the coffee,' Guthrie said.

'I didn't.' Cartwright said dryly.

Guthrie smiled and drifted to the left hand side of the desk. 'Oh, well, that's all right. Then if you haven't been poisoned, how the hell can you be bumped off, here in your own room, under a bright light? And — ' He broke off as the lights suddenly dimmed. 'What's that?'

After a moment's pause the lights came up again.

'What happened?'

'A preliminary test, I should say,' Cartwright said calmly, moving out from the desk and going over to the fireplace. 'Haven't you seen the announcement? Change over to a new grid system. The current may be turned off for a minute.'

Guthrie tapped his forehead with his palm. 'Oh, that, of course! I'd forgotten it was tonight.'

'It's not till nine o'clock, if I remember rightly,' Dr. Morelle said, precise as ever.

Cartwright smiled faintly. 'Nine o'clock. Pure coincidence, of course. But not the kind one relishes when — '

'When did you receive that note?' Dr. Morelle cut in.

'Midday.'

'By post?'

'Pushed under the door.'

'It could have been written this

morning?' Dr. Morelle asked.

Cartwright shrugged. 'I suppose so.'

'After the announcement of the switch-over in the papers?' Dr. Morelle pursued.

'Yes.' Cartwright paused. 'My dear Doctor, I know that in taking this business seriously I'm behaving in an irrational manner . . . '

'Perhaps not quite irrational.'

'But I somehow felt this was an evening when I'd appreciate company,' Cartwright admitted.

Guthrie crossed to the end of the sofa. 'Company! I'd want an army.'

Cartwright smiled gravely, 'You think there may be something in it after all?'

'I admit I don't blame you getting the wind up,' Guthrie said frankly, 'though all you've got to do is lock these two doors and sit tight.'

'You read my thoughts,' Cartwright said. 'It's what I intend to do.' He looked at his watch. 'In exactly twelve minutes from now . . . ' He broke off and glanced towards the hall as Miles appeared in the doorway.

'There's a knock at the front door, sir.'

He hesitated. 'Am I to open it?'

Cartwright glanced uncertainly at Dr, Morelle.

The Doctor nodded. 'I think he may. I have decided to remain.'

Cartwright fished out his key to give to Miles. 'Here; see who it is.'

'I would rather Mr. Guthrie went,' Dr. Morelle said suavely.

Cartwright shrugged and gave Guthrie the key instead. 'As you please.'

As Guthrie left the room. Cartwright smiled grimly at his manservant. 'You are not trusted, Miles. I hope you're duly impressed.'

Miles bowed respectfully and went out. Cartwright dropped into the nearest armchair and looked at Dr. Morelle.

'So you're going to take on the case?'

'I don't particularly believe in the case,' Dr. Morelle said slowly, 'but I've discovered an important thing about you.'

'Which is?'

'That you are afraid.'

Cartwright shrugged. 'I *am* afraid; though, according to you, Doctor, of nothing.'

'You are afraid of something which you have omitted to disclose to me,' Dr. Morelle said coldly. 'I am staying until I know what that is.'

Guthrie appeared at the doorway. 'It's a Miss Frayle,' he smiled.

Dr, Morelle made a resigned gesture and moved behind the desk.

'Does she come in?' Guthrie asked.

'Unless you've a cast-iron plan for preventing her,' the Doctor murmured.

'She is Dr. Morelle's invaluable assistant,' Cartwright offered.

'I have yet to find her equal,' Dr. Morelle admitted ambiguously. 'Show her in.'

Guthrie looked back into the hall. 'Miss Frayle.'

3

Miss Frayle came into the room. She was a fluffy, petite blonde, who looked to be in her late twenties. She wore a dark, rather prim — but not unattractive — dinner-dress. As the men looked at her, she adjusted her horn-rimmed spectacles nervously.

'I do hope I'm not too late.'

Dr. Morelle glanced at his watch. 'Only fifty-two minutes.'

'I went the wrong way round on the Inner Circle,' Miss Frayle said brightly.

'What were you doing on the Inner Circle at all?' Dr. Morelle asked.

'Yes — I know . . . ' Miss Frayle looked at Guthrie. 'Mr. Cartwright?'

Cartwright rose. 'How do you do?'

Miss Frayle spun round to face the speaker. 'Oh! How do you do?'

Cartwright attempted to allay her confusion. 'Mr. Guthrie — Miss Frayle.'

'Good evening.' Guthrie smiled faintly.

'Mr. Guthrie represents the press,' Cartwright explained.

Miss Frayle nodded. 'How nice.'

'Do sit down, Miss Frayle,' Cartwright continued. 'Would you care for some coffee and sandwiches?'

Miss Frayle seated herself on the sofa. 'No, thanks. I'm sure we're going to be far too busy to eat.'

Cartwright moved towards the drinks table. 'How about a drink?' he suggested. 'A spot of brandy?'

'Er . . . ' Miss Frayle hesitated, then caught the look in Dr. Morelle's eyes. 'No, thank you.'

Dr. Morelle addressed Cartwright: 'At nine o'clock precisely, then, you anticipate an attempt at murder — the assailant being one of four persons in the adjoining room?'

Miss Frayle looked up and gave a start. 'Murder? Who's going to be murdered?'

'Mr. Cartwright,' Dr. Morelle said shortly. 'Please don't interrupt.' He sat at the desk, then went on, looking at Cartwright: 'Now, a few details: you propose to remain in this room?'

Cartwright moved nearer the desk. 'I do.'

'Alone, with both doors locked and the windows to the balcony bolted?' Dr. Morelle prompted.

'Yes.'

Guthrie had drifted to the fireplace. 'And, if nothing happens, you'll open the doors and we can all go home?'

'You may,' Cartwright assented.

'Mr. Cartwright,' Miss Frayle said unsteadily. 'I — I think perhaps I would like a brandy.'

Cartwright smiled, and returned to the drinks table. He poured out a drink and brought it across to her.

Miss Frayle took a long sip, her eyes round and fixed on Cartwright.

Dr. Morelle indicated the door to the dining room as Cartwright turned back to him. 'There is no other door from the dining room?'

'No, only French windows into the garden. I locked them myself before I came in.'

'Would you permit Mr. Guthrie to check that?' Dr. Morelle asked sharply.

'Certainly,' Cartwright agreed promptly, then, as Guthrie crossed to the door, he added: 'What about the front door?'

Guthrie halted, and handed back the front door key. 'I locked it again,' he explained, and then went through to the dining room.

Dr. Morelle indicated the door to the hall. 'That door leads to the hall, at the far end of which is the lounge where your guests are now waiting,' he stated.

Cartwright nodded. 'Yes.'

'You will naturally feel happier if that lounge door is also locked at nine o'clock,' Doctor Morelle said.

'I shall insist on it,' Cartwright said firmly.

'Mr. Guthrie has relocked the front door,' Dr. Morelle summarized. 'So at nine o'clock both the lounge and this room will be, to all intents and purposes, hermetically sealed, with your guests in the lounge and you here.'

'Correct,' Cartwright affirmed.

Miss Frayle handed him her empty glass. 'But then how can you possibly be murdered?' she asked.

'That, Miss Frayle, is the jackpot question,' he replied, taking the glass to the drinks table.

Guthrie re-entered from the dining room. 'French windows are locked all right,' he announced. 'No possible chance of anyone getting in that way.'

'Then,' Dr. Morelle instructed, 'if you'd be so good as to lock the door . . . ' As Guthrie complied, he added: 'What about your manservant?'

Cartwright looked back from where he stood near the fireplace. 'Miles? What about him?'

'Where will he be?'

'With all of you in the lounge, of course,' Cartwright replied.

'Look, as a reporter I hate not being in on anything,' Guthrie said earnestly. 'How about letting Dr. Morelle and me stay here? You'd be much safer.'

Cartwright shook his head. 'You'll be the first on the scene. That's the best I can offer.'

'Pity,' Guthrie sighed. 'You know, I find this all rather provoking. Here's something with all the earmarks of a first-class story; the only thing is, it just can't happen.'

'Keep your pencil sharpened,' Cartwright advised enigmatically.

Guthrie smiled. 'Okay. What's it feel like to be five minutes away from being a corpse?'

'Frankly, uncomfortable.' Cartwright paused. 'I have a strange presentiment. An indefinable feeling that these are my last moments on earth. That I am thinking my last thoughts, speaking my last words — and what is more disturbing, enjoying my last brandy.'

'Any theory about which one of them's going to do the job?' Guthrie asked.

'I believe only one of them has the guts.'

'Who?'

Cartwright dodged the question. 'Ask Dr. Morelle.'

'Any other statements? Last words and so on?'

'I believe in capital punishment.' Cartwright looked at his watch. 'And it's four and half minutes to.'

Dr. Morelle rose, indicating to Miss

Frayle the French windows opening on to the balcony outside. 'Fasten the windows, Miss Frayle.'

She got up and went towards the French windows, first deciding to ascertain there was no one outside.

She stopped and pulled one of the curtains aside, and regarded the windows with alarm as Dr. Morelle watched her.

'I — I think I can see from here,' she said timorously.

'You will see better outside,' Dr. Morelle said impatiently. He turned to Cartwright: 'Kindly ring for Miles.'

Cartwright pressed the summoning bell near the fireplace.

Miss Frayle was just nervously stepping on to the balcony when something knocked the windows into her face. She started back with a scream.

Dr. Morelle dashed out on to balcony.

'A body!' Miss Frayle was almost incoherent. 'And a face! The eyes looked straight into mine: they were horrible.'

Guthrie came forward and helped the distraught Miss Frayle into a chair beside the desk.

Outside, Dr. Morelle flashed a pocket torch along the balcony rail.

Cartwright smiled. 'It's only Mr. Smith. He does it deliberately to scare me. Sits on the balcony rail and then jumps.'

Dr. Morelle came back into room. 'Add to the list of suspects, Miss Frayle, one Siamese cat.'

'A cat?' Miss Frayle looked up. 'Oh, but — and I thought it was . . . '

'Don't worry, he won't come into the house,' Cartwright assured her. 'Siamese never do when strangers are about.'

Dr. Morelle was fastening the French windows himself when Miles answered the summons.

'You rang, sir?'

Cartwright nodded to Dr. Morelle, who said: 'I shall require you to accompany Miss Frayle to the lounge and remain there.'

Miss Frayle got unsteadily to her feet.

'Now, sir?' Miles asked.

'Now,' Dr. Morelle said firmly.

Miss Frayle turned to him. 'But aren't you coming, too?'

'No. Mr. Guthrie and I will follow in a moment.'

Miss Frayle looked ruefully at Cartwright. 'I'm — sorry to have been so stupid.'

Cartwright smiled faintly. 'On the contrary, Miss Frayle, I find you a great comfort.'

'Oh, really? Why?'

'Because even if I tried, I couldn't be as scared as you look,' Cartwright said dryly.

'Oh — thank you — that is . . . ' Smiling uncertainly, she went out with Miles.

Dr. Morelle looked at Cartwright, standing by the fireplace. 'When we leave, you will turn the key after us and all entrances to this room will then be locked, with the keys on the inside.'

'That is correct.'

'Then, if these electricity fellows do their stuff, the lights will go out,' Guthrie said.

Dr. Morelle began moving to the door. 'We shall wait, locked in the lounge, until the lights go up again. I shall then unlock the lounge door, cross the hall and knock at this door. In the unlikely event of there being no answer, we shall break in.'

'If there's no answer, you won't have to,' Cartwright remarked, moving back into the centre of the room.

'What do you mean?' Guthrie asked.

'Won't my visitor have left it open? Unless you're suggesting he's clever enough to leave a room with the door locked on the inside. That's rating him higher than I do.'

Dr. Morelle smiled thinly at the unassailable logic. 'I accept the point.'

Cartwright glanced at Guthrie. 'Anything more for the press?'

'Yes. What are you going to do with your last three minutes?'

Cartwright sighed reflectively. 'Ah, of course. The murdered man's last moments. How often, Dr. Morelle, would you like to have known about them? Tonight you shall know them in detail.' He diverted to the drinks table, picked up his brandy and walked slowly round room, down to the fireplace and then back below the sofa. 'I shall take a turn round the room with my cigar and my brandy, glancing idly at familiar objects; smoking, drinking . . . ' Reaching his writing desk, he added: 'I shall then sit at my desk.' He did so. 'That, as near as I can give it, will be my position at the fatal hour.'

'You won't move from there?' Dr. Morelle asked.

'Not once I have sat here. Neither the cigar nor the brandy will leave my hands.'

Dr, Morelle glanced at the reporter. 'I think we have everything. Mr. Guthrie!'

Guthrie crossed to the door as Dr. Morelle gave a final look round the room, 'You will not omit to lock this door?'

Cartwright nodded. 'Trust me.'

'And carry out your movements to the letter?'

'To the letter.'

Going to the door, Dr. Morelle opened it. He remained in the doorway and looked back as Guthrie passed outside.

'With confidence, Mr. Cartwright, *au revoir*.'

'With conviction, Dr. Morelle, *adieu*.'

After Dr. Morelle went out, Cartwright remained seated for a moment at the, desk, smoking his cigar. He put down his drink and crossed to the hall door, locked it and left the key in lock.

He glanced at the clock on the mantelpiece and returned to the desk. Picking up his glass in one hand and with the cigar in the other, he walked slowly round the room, glancing thoughtfully at each object in turn.

Coming back to the desk he sat as before, cigar in his left hand, drink in his right.

The hall clock started striking the quarters. The lights and electric fire slowly dimmed and went out.

The room was in complete darkness except for the glow of Cartwright's cigar. As the hall clock began striking nine, the telephone on the writing desk suddenly rang. For a moment the cigar glow made no move as the ringing continued. Then the cigar glow moved forward.

'Hello? Hello? Who is that?'

There was a sudden deafening bang as a revolver shot was fired in the room.

The telephone receiver fell with a crash to the desk and there was a muffled thump in the darkness as the body of Cartwright slumped forward,

4

Cartwright's study was still in darkness. The sound of footsteps came from the hall outside. The muffled voices of Dr. Morelle and then Guthrie penetrated the locked door, then gave way to a loud banging on the door itself.

The banging became punctuated with the sound of Dr. Morelle's voice: 'Cartwright! Cartwright!'

Other voices came: Evelyn's and Troon's.

'Cartwright! Are you there?'

Abruptly, the door was burst open, just as the lights in the room came back on.

The body of Cartwright was revealed, sprawled across the desk; beside it, the telephone receiver was off its hook.

Dr. Morelle and Guthrie advanced quickly into the room, followed by June Lister. Troon, Evelyn and Forbes remained inside the doorway.

'For God's sake!' Guthrie exclaimed.

'Stay where you are, everyone!' Dr. Morelle snapped, moving forward to the side of the desk. Under his breath he murmured. 'With conviction, Doctor, *adieu*!'

June muttered in a low voice: 'It had to happen . . . '

Dr. Morelle looked towards the hall. 'Miss Frayle!'

'Yes, Doctor,' she called back. 'Coming . . . '

With a muttered 'Excuse me,' Miss Frayle pushed her way past the others in the doorway, She came forward into the room, and stopped in front of the sofa, averting her eyes from the body slumped across the desk.

Dr. Morelle turned to address the room. 'The rest of you may go,' he announced.

'Go?' Forbes was incredulous.

'The front door's locked,' Troon pointed out.

'I will let anyone out . . . who is not prepared to answer questions.' Dr. Morelle looked from one to the other. All remained silent. 'In that case, perhaps you would all wait in the lounge. And, Miles?'

'Sir,' The manservant had followed Miss Frayle, and hovered in the doorway, staring at his late employer.

'Be ready to come, if I ring,' Dr. Morelle instructed.

'Yes, Doctor.'

'That will be all.'

Miles stiffened imperceptibly at this dismissal, then the training of his calling took over, and he turned and went out,

Dr. Morelle looked at the reporter. 'Oh, Mr. Guthrie, you might, perhaps, be interested to observe my investigations.'

'Thank you, Doctor,' Guthrie said quietly. 'I would indeed.'

Dr. Morelle regarded the others, who had not moved. 'You know, I think, where the lounge is.'

They hesitated only momentarily, evidently still shocked by events, then responding to the Doctor's commanding air they too turned and went out. 'And please shut the door,' he called after them.

Miss Frayle and Guthrie stood respectfully as Dr. Morelle turned to look again at the body of Cartwright. Presently he walked slowly round it.

'Shot through the right temple . . . ' he murmured, 'just a minute . . . ' The Doctor crossed to the door of the dining room, unlocked it, and went inside.

A few moments later he returned. 'No one there,' he announced, 'and the French windows still locked on the inside.'

'The key's still on the inside of this door, too,' Guthrie remarked.

'Check those windows,' Dr. Morelle told him.

As Guthrie went to examine the French windows, Dr. Morelle came back to the desk and felt carefully in Cartwright's pockets. He took out certain articles. Watching him, Miss Frayle edged timidly forward, to stand nearer the desk Guthrie came back to join her. 'The room's exactly as we left it,' he announced.

'No one could have come in,' Dr. Morelle said slowly. 'No one could have got out. And Cartwright has been shot through the head.' He looked down at the articles in his hand.

'The key of the front door and the note he read to us.' He looked more closely at the note. 'What do you make of that?' he finished, handing the note to Guthrie.

The reporter scrutinized the note. 'He's scribbled something on it; probably doodling.' He handed it back to Dr. Morelle's outstretched hand.

'Looks like a name,' the Doctor mused. 'Lassegue.' He spoke the name to rhyme with 'vague'. 'Or might it be a place?' He glanced at Guthrie, who shrugged.

Miss Frayle had managed to steel herself to look directly at the body of Cartwright. 'I suppose — he is dead?' she said uneasily.

'If not, he is shamming most convincingly,' Dr. Morelle said dryly.

Miss Frayle wrinkled her brow, 'But, Doctor, how could it have happened?'

'He was shot.'

Miss Frayle gasped, 'Who by?'

'By whom,' Dr. Morelle said coldly. 'If you are proposing to faint, now would be a more convenient time.'

Miss Frayle backed away, and sat down unsteadily on the sofa.

'I think Miss Frayle would be happier if we removed the body,' Dr. Morelle said, glancing at Guthrie

He came up to the desk, and together they raised Cartwright from the chair. They carried the body out into the dining room.

At a slight noise from the hall doorway, Miss Frayle looked up from where she sat unhappily on the sofa.

'Excuse me,' said Miles.

'You gave me a start. What do you want?'

Miles stepped into the room. 'Dr. Morelle said I was to be about in case he rang.'

'Well, he hasn't. No one has.'

'That's all right, madam. Only I'm here if they do.' He gave a slight nod, and went out.

A few moments later the two men returned from the dining room, Dr. Morelle in the lead. He glanced back. 'Close the door.' Guthrie did so.

Dr. Morelle moved to the centre of the room and looked about him. 'No one could have come in. No one could have got out. And Cartwright has been shot through the head.'

Miss Frayle nodded. 'That proves it.'

'Proves what?'

Miss Frayle spread her hands. 'That it's a clear case of suicide.'

'There is only one thing against it,' Dr. Morelle said patiently. 'I do not see any revolver.' He gestured at the floor surrounding the desk. 'In a case of suicide, it is usually apparent.'

Miss Frayle rose, unfazed. 'Oh, but Doctor, there *is* a revolver! The one he put in the drawer of his desk.'

Dr. Morelle inclined his head. 'I am deeply obliged,' he said dryly. He opened the drawer and took out the revolver. He opened the chamber and inspected the weapon.

'It has not been fired. It would, in any event, be a noteworthy feat to shoot oneself through the head and then return the revolver to its customary place.'

Miss Frayle looked deflated. 'I see what you mean, Doctor.'

Guthrie said: 'But if no one has been in or out, and Cartwright didn't shoot himself . . .'

Dr. Morelle placed the revolver in his pocket. 'That is what we have to find out.'

Guthrie stared at him. 'We? How about the police?'

'They will be given an opportunity later.'

'Later!' Guthrie came nearer the desk. 'But look here, you can't do that. It's our duty . . . '

Dr. Morelle looked at him levelly. 'It is our duty to apprehend a murderer. After I've had the pleasure of unmasking him, the police will then be called.'

'And suppose you don't find him?' Guthrie challenged.

Dr. Morelle shrugged. 'The police would not have found him either; and it would have been a waste of their valuable time to have called them.' He glanced to where the telephone receiver was hanging. 'Our friend was on the telephone. Rather an odd time to make a call, don't you agree?'

'He may have received one,' Guthrie said hesitantly.

Using his handkerchief, Dr. Morelle carefully lifted the receiver.

The telephone was the old-fashioned type with a mouthpiece and receiver separate.

Miss Frayle moved up to the desk, alongside Guthrie. 'What a silly, old-fashioned phone.'

Guthrie shrugged. 'You're lucky to get any sort these days. We still live in austere times.'

Dr. Morelle flashed the receiver hook up and down for a moment, then dialled 'O' for the operator.

'The line's dead,' he announced.

Guthrie came forward to the desk, and taking Dr. Morelle's handkerchief to handle the receiver, listened a moment, then replaced the receiver on the desk. 'That means the line must have been cut.'

'Or out of order,' Dr. Morelle said.

'Anyway, he couldn't have received any call,' Guthrie said emphatically.

Dr. Morelle reflected a moment.

'Mr. Guthrie, on second thoughts tell the others they need not stay in the lounge. Perhaps they would care for Miles to make them some coffee.'

Guthrie nodded and moved towards

door. 'Would you like some, Doctor?'

'No, thanks.'

'Miss Frayle?'

'Ye — er — ' Then at a look from Dr. Morelle, she finished: 'No, thanks.'

After Guthrie went out, Dr. Morelle walked slowly away from the desk, then turned and regarded it thoughtfully. Returning to the desk, he began to examine the articles on it.

'Dr. Morelle, I have an idea,' Miss Frayle began. Dr, Morelle glanced at her, and picked up a piece of paper. 'Couldn't Mr. Cartwright . . . that is to say . . . if . . . But then, of course, he'd have to . . . unless . . . No . . . no, I'm afraid not.'

'Thank you, all the same,' Dr. Morelle murmured dryly. He was studying a broken pair of spectacles, which he had found beneath the paper. He held the broken pieces up to the light.

'Most interesting,' he mused.

Guthrie returned to the room. 'No one seems to want any coffee.' He closed the door and looked at Dr. Morelle enquiringly.

'At eight fifty-eight,' Dr. Morelle said, fingering the spectacles, 'Cartwright was living. Last seen sitting at his desk with lighted cigar in left hand, glass in right.' He paused. 'At one minute past nine he was dead, with the telephone receiver off its hook, lying on some letters beneath which was a pair of broken spectacles.'

'Broken!' Guthrie exclaimed. 'What d'you make of that?'

'The receiver was dropped,' Dr. Morelle said briefly.

'When he was shot?' supplied Miss Frayle.

'Exactly. But the cigar and the glass were put down. By the way, you observe the cigar . . . '

Guthrie came forward to the right of the desk, Miss Frayle following and looking over his shoulder.

'Resting on a paperweight,' Miss Frayle observed.

'Quite remarkable!' Dr. Morelle said dryly. 'Anything else?'

Guthrie looked again. 'A pretty healthy ash.'

'About half an inch long,' Dr. Morelle agreed,

Miss Frayle had one of her inspirations:

'Doctor, that means it wasn't put down in a hurry!'

'Brilliant, Miss Frayle,' Dr. Morelle smiled cynically.

Guthrie frowned. 'I don't quite get it.'

'Miss Frayle will expound,' Dr. Morelle said suavely.

'Well, I — that is — it wasn't put down in a hurry.'

'You have already stated that,' Dr. Morelle said dryly. He looked at Guthrie. 'It was put down calmly and deliberately for a purpose.'

'To use the phone?' Guthrie suggested.

'Possibly. It was also put down in the dark.'

Guthrie looked his puzzlement.

'Here,' Dr. Morelle explained, 'we have an ashtray with rest provided for cigar or cigarette. In our presence, and no doubt scores of times before, Cartwright has placed his cigar on that rest. Why, on this occasion, go out of his way to balance it precariously on a paperweight? For one reason: he put it down in the dark, mistaking it for the ashtray.'

'All right,' Guthrie said. 'He puts the

cigar down in the dark . . . '

'To use the telephone, Dr. Morelle stated. Guthrie nodded. 'It follows, then, that he got on to the telephone in the dark. Our first discovery.'

'What's important about that?' Guthrie asked, puzzled.

Dr. Morelle smiled faintly. 'Have you ever tried dialling in the dark?'

'I have,' Miss Frayle said brightly. 'It's not a bit difficult. You just slide your finger round the dial and count, one, two, three, four . . . '

'And how about the letters?' Dr. Morelle asked patiently.

'They're easy. They go ABC, DEF, GHI . . . '

'What's the number with ABC?'

'One, of course,' Miss Frayle answered promptly.

'You're wrong,' Dr. Morelle said sharply, 'it's two. Take it from me, there is only one number you could get in the dark.'

Guthrie pulled up a chair and sat down near the desk. 'You mean O?'

Dr. Morelle nodded. 'That, my dear

Guthrie, is the discovery. Cartwright could not have rung any particular person; only the exchange . . . Do not despise these little details. They crop up later.'

Miss Frayle smiled. 'It's the little things that count in a case like this. The unnoticed matchstick, the stubbed-out cigarette . . . the stubbed-out cigarette, the — er — the unnoticed matchstick — ' She broke off confusedly and seated herself on the sofa.

Dr. Morelle ignored her and glanced at Guthrie. 'So Cartwright telephoned the exchange. What happens next? The murderer, by means best known to himself, enters a locked room and shoots him.'

Guthrie nodded. 'Yes.'

'Ten seconds later the lights go up.'

'And in those ten seconds,' Guthrie extrapolated incredulously, 'the murderer's cleared out, leaving the doors locked on the inside, and got to the lounge without anyone having noticed him leaving!'

'Apparently,' Dr. Morelle mused.

'You think that possible?'

'It is a fact with which we are faced.'

Miss Frayle got up from the sofa. 'But surely, Doctor, the impossible can't be a fact?'

'You yourself are living proof to the contrary,' Dr. Morelle said dryly. Miss Frayle flushed, and sat down again. He looked at Guthrie. 'The body in the next room is evidence of the impossible and when you are confronted with the impossible there remains only one course to take.'

'What's that?'

'Proceed as if it were possible; and you may come to something.'

Guthrie smiled. 'If it's only an asylum.'

Dr. Morelle leaned forward in his seat behind the desk. 'We have, in fact, arrived somewhere already: a profound and startling fact I had overlooked.'

'What?' Guthrie asked.

'That Cartwright was shot with perfect aim clean through the temple in pitch darkness. Does that not strike you as remarkable?'

'It strikes me as — ' Guthrie began.

Dr. Morelle interrupted, 'You may argue, of course, that a man who projects himself through keyholes is unlikely to have his aim affected by the dark. Stand at the hall door, would you, Miss Frayle? And Mr. Guthrie,' he pointed, 'stand over there.'

Miss Frayle crossed to the hall door, and Guthrie rose and went to where he had been directed.

'Cartwright sat here, so, the receiver in his left hand. The murderer, who had just come in, was standing in the doorway, where Miss Frayle is now.' He looked at Guthrie. 'Will you turn out the lights? I want to look at this in darkness.'

Guthrie turned out the lights with the switch by the door. The room was again plunged into complete darkness.

'Miss Frayle,' Dr. Morelle called, 'would you mind taking aim?'

'Aim, Doctor?'

'Point at where you imagine my head to be . . . Are you aiming?'

'Straight at you, Doctor.'

'Now, Guthrie,' Dr. Morelle instructed, 'if you would switch on the lights again . . . '

As Guthrie turned up the lights, Miss Frayle, her eyes closed, was seen to be aiming at a point nowhere near to Dr. Morelle.

'I do not think I was in any great danger,' he smiled.

Miss Frayle opened her eyes. 'Isn't it funny the difference darkness makes? Now, I remember . . . '

'Half a moment,' Guthrie interrupted. 'The light of the cigar in his mouth: that would have provided a target — ' He broke off. 'Ah, but we know from the ash that it had been put down.'

Dr. Morelle smiled faintly. 'You see how these little details crop up.' He glanced at Miss Frayle. 'All right, William Tell, relax.'

Miss Frayle lowered her hand.

'Now, if he did not shoot from the door, he must have come closer,' Dr. Morelle paused and looked at Guthrie. 'Turn out the lights again.'

Guthrie did so. Dr. Morelle's voice sounded in the darkness: 'Miss Frayle, when I give you the word I want you to move as quickly as you can to the top of the desk. Are you ready?'

'Yes, Doctor.'

'Move!'

Seconds later there sounded the crash of a falling body.

Miss Frayle was revealed in the light of Dr. Morelle's powerful torch sprawling headforemost over the left arm of the sofa.

'Not the most convenient position for murder,' Dr. Morelle commented suavely.

Guthrie turned on the lights again. 'You all right, Miss Frayle?'

'Yes, thank you,' Miss Frayle said, breathing hard.

'It's unlikely, then, he came from the door,' Dr. Morelle stated. 'It's unlikely he aimed from the door.'

Miss Frayle struggled to her feet. 'If I may be allowed to make a suggestion . . .'

Dr. Morelle ignored her and spoke to Guthrie: 'But he must have done one or the other.'

'He could have stayed at the door . . .' Miss Frayle cut in.

'We have already decided, Miss Frayle . . .'

' . . . and used a torch,' Miss Frayle

finished triumphantly.

There was a moment's pause. Dr. Morelle looked at Guthrie and gave a slightly embarrassed cough. He handed the torch to Guthrie. 'Stand by the door. Miss Frayle, the lights.'

Guthrie crossed to the door, then Miss Frayle turned out the lights.

'Shine it on the desk,' Dr. Morelle instructed.

Guthrie shone the torch on the desk. Dr. Morelle sat framed in the circle of light.

'A somewhat better target. Now let's have Cartwright's exact position.' Dr. Morelle picked up the receiver and leaned forward to the mouthpiece.

'Why leaning forward?' Guthrie was curious. 'Couldn't he have picked up the telephone and sat back with it?'

'That is just the point. Why does he not want us to know that the line was cut? Why has he risked his neck to put it right?'

'And you think that Miss Wells . . . '

'She was Cartwright's secretary for six months. I want to know how and where that telephone could be cut. I want to know ... ' Dr. Morelle broke off as Evelyn Wells came in, followed by Miss Frayle, who seated herself in an armchair

The Doctor pulled a chair beside the desk and moved it to a more central position. 'Come and sit down.'

Evelyn hesitated a moment, then sat in the chair.

'Are you feeling a little better?'

'A little, thank you.'

'This has been a great shock to you,' Dr. Morelle said quietly, as he stood facing her.

'To all of us,' Evelyn agreed.

'And — a relief?'

'Frankly, yes.'

Dr. Morelle nodded. 'Because now, what happened here three nights ago will not be made public?'

Evelyn hesitated. 'Yes.'

'Are you prepared to tell me what that was?'

Evelyn tightened her lips. 'No.'

'It is a waste of time my asking any of you?'

'Yes.'

87

'Very well.' Dr. Morelle moved towards the desk, then turned, facing the seated woman. 'You were Mr. Cartwright's secretary for six months?'

'Yes,' Evelyn assented.

'In this house?'

'Yes.'

'What made you leave?' Dr. Morelle asked sharply.

Evelyn shrugged. 'Anyone would leave Cartwright after a time — whether as his secretary or anything else.'

'While you were here you got to know the house pretty well?'

'Naturally.'

'At what point does the telephone line enter?'

'It comes in near the switchboard,' Evelyn answered promptly,

'What switchboard?'

'The one in the hall. You see, there are three phones. The switchboard controls them.'

Dr. Morelle walked behind the desk and sat down. He made a pyramid of his hands and leaned forward. 'Would you be more explicit?'

'Well, there's one phone in the hall, one in the lounge and this one. When an outside call comes through, the hall phone rings. If it's for the lounge, you turn the switchboard pointer to 'lounge'; if it's for the study, you turn it to 'study'.

Guthrie, who had been listening intently, murmured, 'Oh, I see.'

Evelyn gave him a brief glance then looked back to Dr. Morelle who was regarding her thoughtfully. 'There's also a cross line 'lounge to study'. That is, lounge to here. For instance, if someone in the lounge wanted to speak to you now — '

'What would he have to do?' Dr. Morelle asked sharply.

'As long as he was connected to you on the switchboard, he would only have to lift the receiver.'

'And this phone would ring?'

'Yes.'

Dr. Morelle leaned forward slightly. 'I am going to take you into my confidence. When we came into this room after the murder, we were unable to call the exchange. How do you explain that?'

Evelyn shrugged. 'It's not surprising. You weren't through to the exchange.'

Guthrie and Miss Frayle looked at her in surprise. Guthrie seated himself on the arm of the sofa.

'How do you know?' Dr. Morelle asked levelly.

'Because just before nine o'clock, that's just before you and Mr. Guthrie joined us in the lounge, I had a desperate idea of calling the police,' Evelyn admitted. 'I went to the phone in the hall. Major Troon came after me and stopped me, but I did happen to notice that the pointer was at 'lounge to study'.

'Lounge to study?' Dr. Morelle repeated.

'Immediately afterwards, you both joined us all in the lounge and locked the door.'

'Then,' Dr. Morelle said slowly, 'so far as you know, the pointer must still be at 'lounge to study'.

'Yes.'

'And if it is, it is impossible for me to speak to the exchange now.'

'Quite impossible,' Evelyn agreed.

'Well, I have just spoken to them,' Dr.

Morelle said blandly,

Evelyn stared at him blankly. 'But, you can't have.'

'I have.'

Evelyn frowned, 'Then somebody must have changed it.'

Dr. Morelle's eyes gleamed. 'Exactly.'

Evelyn stood up and regarded Dr. Morelle defiantly. 'I'm sorry, Dr. Morelle, but it can't have been changed.'

Dr. Morelle raised an eyebrow. 'What makes you so certain?'

'Because when Mr. Guthrie came into the lounge with your message I thought I was going to faint and wanted some air. I came and stood in the hall and I've been there the whole time till you sent for me.'

Miss Frayle got up. 'It's true. I found her there.'

'I had a clear view of the switchboard the whole time,' Evelyn said firmly. 'I'm prepared to swear that no one went near it.'

Dr. Morelle looked at her sharply. 'Now this is of vital importance. Was the switch still at 'lounge to study?'

'Oh, yes, I think so.' She hesitated. 'I

don't know . . . But I do know no one's been near that board while I was there.'

Dr. Morelle sighed. 'Yes, you think so; no, you don't know. All you do know is that nobody went near it while you were there. Thank you.'

Evelyn began to get up to leave.

'I haven't finished.' Evelyn nervously resumed her seat. 'You left the dinner table this evening saying you weren't feeling very well,' Dr. Morelle resumed. 'What did you do before the others joined you?'

'I just sat here.'

Dr. Morelle raised his eyebrows. 'You just sat here? But not before you had taken Cartwright's revolver from his desk.'

'Yes,' Evelyn admitted hesitantly.

Dr. Morelle stood up. 'So you meant to kill him?'

'No, no, I only meant to frighten him.'

'You meant to kill Cartwright,' Dr. Morelle went on relentlessly. 'Will you tell me why?'

'But I didn't, I didn't!'

Dr. Morelle came around the desk.

'Then let me tell you. You meant to kill Cartwright, not only because of what happened the other night, but because for some time he had been threatening to tell Major Troon something you did not want him to know.'

'There's not a word of truth in what you're saying,' Evelyn protested angrily. 'It's a lie!'

'I suggest it is you who are lying.' Dr. Morelle hardened his voice. 'You didn't go into the hall before the murder to ring the police; you didn't go into the hall after the murder because you felt faint; you went into the hall to change the switchboard pointer.'

'I didn't,' Evelyn said desperately, 'I didn't! Why should I?'

'Why on earth should you . . . ' Dr. Morelle said slowly. His eyes rested searchingly on her for a moment. Then: 'All right. Ask Miles to come in, will you?'

Evelyn rose unsteadily, then turned and went out.

Miss Frayle settled back on the sofa. 'Well, that's cooked her goose. She's lying. She changed the thing herself or she's shielding someone who did.'

Dr. Morelle leaned against the front of the desk, and smiled faintly. 'Then she is shielding him very badly. The murderer risked his neck to conceal what she told us: that the pointer was at 'lounge to study'. And why? Because it would tell us an all-important fact. That Cartwright never made any call at all. He *received* one, and it came from the lounge.'

Guthrie frowned. 'From the lounge?'

Dr. Morelle nodded. 'Which was connected with this phone. The light is breaking, Guthrie. The murderer lifts the receiver in the lounge and the phone rings here. Cartwright answers it. When the murderer reaches this room, he knows Cartwright's head will be in a fixed position, close to the mouthpiece.'

'Yes, but that doesn't tell us how he got out of the lounge,' Guthrie pointed out. 'And how he got in here. And how he got out again. And, if that girl wasn't lying, who changed the board and when?' He spread his hands and shrugged. 'The whole thing doesn't make sense.'

'It is beginning to.' Dr. Morelle

murmured, taking a chair at the right of the desk. 'Who besides Miss Wells knew the working of that board?'

'Well, I suppose, Miles,' Guthrie answered.

'And who besides Miss Wells would know that this phone was fixed to the desk?'

'Miles,' Guthrie said.

Dr. Morelle leaned forward. 'And tell me one thing more. Who was sitting in the lounge on the piano stool next to the telephone?'

Before anyone could answer, Miles spoke from the doorway. 'You wanted to see me, Doctor?'

Dr. Morelle got up and moved behind the desk. 'Come in, Miles.'

The manservant came into the room, closing the door behind him. He hesitated, looking round the room.

'Mr. Cartwright's body is in the dining room,' Dr. Morelle told him.

Miles advanced into the room. 'I know, sir,' he said quietly.

'How do you know?' Dr. Morelle snapped.

Miss Frayle rose. 'Oh, he was here before.'

'When?'

'When you were removing it.'

Dr. Morelle scowled. 'Why was I not informed?'

Miss Frayle shrugged. 'I didn't think it was important.'

'There are criminals at large today,' Dr. Morelle said acidly, 'who owe their liberty to your idea of what is important.' Miss Frayle flushed slightly, and sat down again,

'I merely looked in to see if I was wanted,' Miles explained.

'Why was that telephone fixed to the desk?' Dr. Morelle asked him.

'The telephone?'

'We thought you might know,' Guthrie put in.

'That is,' Dr. Morelle added, 'unless you have only just recently joined Mr. Cartwright's service?'

'Oh no, I've been with him four years. I joined him in South America.'

'I've always wanted to go to South America,' Miss Frayle said brightly.

Dr. Morelle ignored her. 'Why was that telephone fixed to the desk?'

'To save it from being knocked over,' Miles answered promptly.

'Knocked over?' Guthrie asked, puzzled.

'Being an old-fashioned type. It was here when Mr. Cartwright took over the house,' Miles explained. 'Mr. Smith, the Siamese cat, was always jumping on to the desk and knocking the phone over, so Mr. Cartwright thought it would be convenient for it to be fixed in one place all the time.'

'When was it done?' Dr. Morelle questioned.

'Oh, more than three months ago.'

'And who else knew about it?'

Miles shrugged. 'Well, naturally anyone who's been to this room since.'

'Any of those there tonight, for instance?' Dr. Morelle suggested.

'Any of them, yes,' Miles admitted. 'They've been here several times.'

'Thank you.' Dr. Morelle strolled over towards the fireplace, then paused to regard the impassive manservant keenly. 'Miss Wells has just been explaining to us the workings of the switchboard.'

'Oh, yes.'

'She says there is a connection between this room and the lounge.'

Miles nodded. 'There is, yes.'

'And that it is possible, by lifting the receiver in the lounge, to ring the telephone here?'

'Yes, sir. If the switchboard is at 'lounge to study'.'

'Quite,' Dr. Morelle nodded. 'Have you used that combination at all today?'

'I have not,' Miles replied flatly.

'At no time?'

'At no time.'

'Do you know of anyone else who has?' Dr. Morelle questioned.

'No one.' Miles frowned slightly. 'Why?'

'It was used after dinner?' Guthrie put in.

Miles regarded him blankly. 'After dinner!'

Dr. Morelle moved forward and regarded the manservant levelly. 'Half a minute before Mr. Cartwright was killed . . . '

' . . . he received a call,' Guthrie added.

'From the lounge,' Dr. Morelle finished.

The manservant appeared bewildered. 'From the lounge! But it's impossible. We were all sitting there. You, Miss Frayle and Mr . . . '

Guthrie stood up and drifted towards the fire. 'At the time of the call the lounge was in darkness.'

'But even so,' Miles protested, 'no one knew about the switchboard.'

'Except,' Dr. Morelle corrected, 'Miss Wells, and you.'

'You were sitting next to the telephone, weren't you?' Guthrie said sharply.

'What are you getting at?' Miles faltered.

'He's only asking a question,' Miss Frayle commented, becoming affected by the inquisitorial atmosphere.

Miles looked about him, then sank down into the nearest chair. 'I know nothing, I tell you.'

'All right,' Dr. Morelle said gently. 'For the present I believe you.' He paused, then: 'During the darkness, were you aware of any movement in the lounge?'

'Only when you came over to the piano,' Miles said.

'When would you say that was?' Dr. Morelle questioned.

Miles reflected. 'I should say about fifteen seconds after the lights went out.'

'How did you know it was me?'

Miles shrugged. 'I thought it must be. You gave orders no one else was to move.'

'And you heard me by the piano?' Dr. Morelle mused.

'I thought I saw something, too,' Miles added,

'I never saw anything,' Miss Frayle put in.

'That's not evidence,' Dr. Morelle said acidly.

'A curious little green light,' Miles said hesitantly. 'Just for a moment. It might have been a luminous watch.' He shrugged. 'That's all I can tell you.'

Dr. Morelle returned behind the desk. 'You have been extremely helpful. You see, *I never left my position at the door.*'

Miles became agitated. 'You don't believe me. You think I'm making the whole thing up!'

'You're doing it very well,' Guthrie commented sarcastically,

'I'm telling the truth, I swear it.'

'And I have said I believe you,' Dr. Morelle said quietly, resuming the seat behind the desk. 'This person you think you heard by the piano: suppose he was the murderer and did ring Mr. Cartwright in here. What would he have to do next?'

'Unlock two doors.'

'Are there any spare keys, Miles, to the doors in this house?'

'None.'

'Have any ever been made?' Dr. Morelle pressed.

'Not to my knowledge.'

Miss Frayle stood up excitedly. 'There's something, Doctor, you've overlooked. Someone could have taken a key away and had it duplicated.'

Dr. Morelle inclined his head. 'It is time I retired,' he said dryly.

'But I lock up every night,' Miles objected. 'I'd notice if it had gone.'

'In fact,' Guthrie said challengingly, 'the only person who could have had a key made is yourself. Things don't look too good for you. You had the run of the murdered man's room. You knew the workings of the switchboard. You were sitting next to the telephone. You could have had keys duplicated . . . '

Miles bristled. 'Look here, I'm not going to stand it. I'm not, do you hear? I'm not going to face the music for a thing I know nothing about!'

'Why should you?' Guthrie murmured.

'I'm going to speak.' Miles glared around him, then faced Dr. Morelle, 'There was something Mr. Cartwright didn't tell you tonight. The real reason why he was afraid.'

Dr. Morelle nodded. 'I have been waiting to hear it. What was he afraid of?'

'Someone named Lassegue.'

'Lassegue!' Guthrie exclaimed.

'That was the name on the note,' Miss Frayle said excitedly. 'You remember, Doctor, the one he doodled?'

'My memory functions, too,' Dr, Morelle said coldly, and Miss Frayle sank back into her armchair. He handed the note to Miles. 'That name?'

The manservant looked at the note.

'Yes, Doctor, that name.'

'And who is Lassegue?' Dr. Morelle asked, taking the note back.

'It was someone he had never seen. He didn't even know whether it was a man or a woman . . . ' He hesitated, then: 'I don't know whether I should be telling you all this. But I'm in a spot myself and . . . '

'Go on,' Dr, Morelle encouraged.

'Mr. Cartwright wasn't everything he should have been. There wasn't much in South America he wasn't mixed up in, and most of it was pretty shady. Five years ago he worked a job with a man called Lassegue. Things went wrong, someone got killed. Cartwright saved his own skin by sending Lassegue to the chair.'

'Nice work,' Guthrie commented, seating himself.

'He thought he'd heard the last of it,' Miles resumed. 'For a long time he had. Then a few weeks ago news reached him that someone named Lassegue was in London, looking for him.'

'A relation of the dead man?' Dr. Morelle murmured.

Miles nodded. 'He knew there had been a son or daughter who was in the States at the time of Lassegue's death. It had taken this person five years to catch up with him.'

'How did he react to the news?' Dr. Morelle questioned sharply.

'Mr. Cartwright was a fatalist,' Miles said quietly. 'He believed whoever it was would get what they came for.'

'Tonight?' Miss Frayle gasped.

'Yes.'

'What makes you think so?' Dr. Morelle asked.

'When he showed me that note this morning he said: 'It's unsigned, but the signature is Lassegue'.'

'I see,' Dr, Morelle mused. 'One more question. How did he know Lassegue was in London?'

'He had contacts, South American friends. So have I. One in particular I may be seeing tomorrow. I think he might tell me something.'

'Why not tonight? There's a phone on the desk.' Dr. Morelle indicated the instrument.

Miles hesitated. 'He's not on the phone. I couldn't reach him tonight.'

Dr. Morelle regarded him closely for a moment, then shrugged. 'Very well, Miles. You may go.'

'Thank you, Doctor.'

After the manservant had left, Guthrie got up and began to pace slowly about. 'Well, for Pete's sake! Just when we'd got this whole case pinned on to four people in the next room, along comes someone called Lassegue.'

'That does not dispose of the next room,' Dr. Morelle corrected him.

'Why not?' Miss Frayle asked, surprised.

'Because the note which threatened Cartwright could only have been written by one of them.'

'Oh. That's true,' Miss Frayle admitted,

'But we can't have it both ways,' Guthrie declared. 'Either it's one of them, or Lassegue.'

'It has obviously not occurred to you that one of them may be Lassegue,' Dr. Morelle said quietly.

'One of them! But Doctor, that's not

possible,' Miss Frayle protested.

'Why not?'

'Well, the note says nothing about a father being electrocuted.'

Dr. Morelle made a despairing gesture, at which Miss Frayle, who had stood up in her excitement, promptly sat down again. He glanced at the reporter. 'Mr. Guthrie, please!'

Guthrie addressed Miss Frayle in a kindly tone. 'The note suggested blackmail, Miss Frayle, because it would tend to incriminate three other persons.'

'Make it simpler,' Dr. Morelle said impatiently.

'One of those four is the guilty party, but his or her real name may be Lassegue.'

'Well, my name's Troon and I'd like to go home.' The voice came suddenly, from the doorway.

Dr. Morelle turned to Miss Frayle. 'Call a taxi for Major Troon.'

Miss Frayle obediently rose and moved towards the door,

Troon was surprised. 'You've no objection?'

'So long as Miss Wells remains,' Dr. Morelle said quietly.

Troon came forward angrily. 'Now look here, what have you got against her?'

'A more interesting question: have you ever been in South America?' Dr. Morelle regarded him calmly.

Troon frowned. 'No.'

'Miss Wells?'

'No.' Troon was emphatic.

Guthrie looked at him keenly. 'When did you first meet Cartwright?'

'About three months ago. Miss Wells introduced us when she was his secretary.'

'Any idea when Forbes met him?' Guthrie pursued.

'About six months ago.'

'What about June Lister?' Guthrie asked.

'They met in Rio,' Troon conceded.

Miss Frayle returned to the sofa. 'It's such a heavenly place. 'I had a postcard from there only the other day . . . Oh. Rio!'

'Miss Frayle's geography is a little slow,' Dr. Morelle commented.

'What was she doing in Rio?' Guthrie probed.

'She'd been in Hollywood, filming. Her last picture was on location in Brazil. The unit broke up there and she travelled back to England with Cartwright. But if you want to know anything about her, why not ask her yourself.' He seated himself on the end of the sofa,

Dr. Morelle nodded to Miss Frayle, who rose and went out.

'But I'll give you a word of advice.' Troon resumed. 'June may, for all I know, have killed Cartwright. Whether she did or not, she's unlikely to be helpful.'

Dr. Morelle smiled thinly. 'I'll bear that in mind.' The dining room door suddenly gave a click and opened a few inches. Troon immediately rose and stared intently at the door. 'What's the matter?' Dr. Morelle asked.

'Who — who's in there?' Troon faltered.

'No one,' Dr. Morelle stated.

'You're lying,' Troon said thickly.

'Only Cartwright's body,' Guthrie said dryly.

'But didn't you see, the door opened?'

Guthrie crossed quickly to the door

and went into the dining room as Troon remained staring at the door.

He returned a few moments later and came over to the left side of the desk.

'Only Cartwright,' he announced.

'The door could not have been properly closed,' Dr. Morelle suggested.

'You see, Doctor — it's what happened the other night,' Troon said unsteadily.

Dr. Morelle raised his eyebrows. 'The other night?'

'Yes. The night Cartwright threatened us with blackmail,' Troon explained. 'The others had gone to get a taxi. I was alone with Cartwright here. I was standing just there,' — he pointed. 'He'd got a revolver. Over his shoulder I saw that door open a few inches.'

'What did you do?' Dr. Morelle asked sharply.

'Cartwright said it was Mr. Smith, the Siamese. He told me to look for myself.'

'Did you?' Guthrie asked.

'There was no one there, but the French windows were open.'

'On to the garden?' Guthrie said.

'The garden runs down to the road.'

Troon pointed out.

'You say the others had gone ahead. Could it not have been one of them?' Dr. Morelle asked.

Troon hesitated. 'It could have been. Though I can't see why they should want to eavesdrop — ' He broke off as June Lister appeared.

'I should think not indeed! Very bad manners.' She came forward to the fireside. 'Well, Philip, what have you been saying? We ought to agree.'

'He's been saying that you are unlikely to be helpful,' Dr. Morelle said. 'Is that so?'

June turned to him and smiled. 'I'm sure, Doctor, you wouldn't get that impression.'

'I accept the challenge,' Dr. Morelle said quietly.

Miss Frayle came back into the room, looking flustered. 'I'm sorry, but I can't find her anywhere . . . Oh!' She broke off as she caught sight of the woman she had been fruitlessly seeking.

'I was on the right-hand side of the door, dear, as you came out,' June said sweetly.

Guthrie frowned. 'Then you *were* listening.'

'Mr. Guthrie!' she reproved, seating herself on the sofa. 'A woman never listens, she overhears. I'm at your service, Doctor.'

'Major Troon, would you mind?' Dr. Morelle asked meaningfully.

Troon hesitated. 'June . . . '

'Don't worry, Philip. This is well within my range.'

As Troon left the room, Dr. Morelle glanced at the reporter. 'Mr. Guthrie, you will oblige me by testing the shortest time it takes to reach the dining room windows from the front door, via the garden. Here is the key.'

'Sure.' Guthrie accepted it.

'And I would prefer that Miss Lister did not hear the answer.'

Guthrie went out. 'I'm flattered and intrigued,' June commented.

Dr. Morelle looked at Miss Frayle, waiting for her to go. She remained where she was, her eyes on the actress.

'Miss Frayle,' Dr. Morelle said.

'Yes, Doctor?'

'Would you be kind enough to close the door . . . ?'

With a triumphant smile at June Miss Frayle got up and went to the door

'From the other side,' Dr. Morelle finished dryly.

Miss Frayle turned, giving him an angry look. June smiled at her sweetly. Miss Frayle sniffed and went out, closing the door firmly behind her.

'Seriously, Doctor, you're wasting your time with me,' June said.

Dr. Morelle crossed the room and sat on the arm of the sofa. 'I seldom waste time, Miss Lister; never with a woman.'

June smiled. 'Now that is a remark that can be taken in two ways.'

'The first is correct.' Doctor Morelle took an earring from his pocket. 'Would this earring happen to be yours?'

June looked at it, then nodded. 'Yes, it is. I'm so glad. Where did you find it?'

Doctor Morelle indicated a corner of the room. 'Over there.'

'I must have dropped it before dinner.'

'Where is the other one?' Dr. Morelle asked. There was an awkward pause.

June's hand went involuntarily to her ear. 'Or is it the fashion now to dine out with a single earring?' he added dryly.

June hesitated. 'I — I must have been wearing them three nights ago.'

'I think that might be nearer the truth,' Dr. Morelle said, rising.

'And I dropped it in this room.'

Dr. Morelle moved to the fireplace. 'When you and the others were here with Cartwright?'

'Yes.'

'How long were you all here?'

June reflected. 'About a quarter of an hour.'

'You remained in this room the whole time?'

'We did. Any more questions?'

'Only those you are unlikely to answer.'

'Thank you.' June rose as if to go towards the door, then returned to the end of the sofa. 'I had nothing to do with Brian's death, if that's what you're after.'

'You had something to do with his life.'

'Who gave you that idea?'

'Cartwright,' Dr. Morelle said briefly. June remained silent. 'He said, if I remember rightly, that 'in all great loves, one tires before the other'.'

'He'd got something there.'

'And he was the one to tire.'

'That's a lie,' June flared, 'a cheap, rotten lie.'

'He is hardly in a position to defend himself.'

June tightened her lips. 'If he was, he'd lie his way out of it; out of anything; out of the filthy trick he played on us three nights ago; and where it landed him.'

Dr. Morelle smiled thinly. 'No flowers by general consent. You met him in Brazil, you came back to England with him.'

'Because of another lie,' June said bitterly. 'He was putting some money in a play in London and he said there was a part for me.'

'And was there?'

'Yes, but it wasn't in the play. As soon as I found that out I walked out on him. And that's the dreary little story.'

Dr. Morelle leaned on the end of the end of the sofa. 'It will not, I hope, distress you to learn that I do not believe a word of it. May I tell you my version?

You met him in Rio. You were attracted by his charm, *savoir faire*, the ease with which he moved through life. You fell in love with him. You were going to be married. When you got back to London, you discovered what others had learned before you: that you had already given him all that he wanted. From that moment your love turned to bitterness, your bitterness to hatred, the hatred you have shown tonight. But beneath it all the love you felt for him is still there.'

'Thank you for a most romantic version.' June smiled dismissively. 'Fortunately for me, mine is the true one.'

'That is all you have to say?'

'That is all.'

Dr. Morelle regarded her for a moment, then gestured resignedly, 'A pity. And so his latest eccentricity has failed.'

'What do you mean?'

'Everything that has happened tonight was a deep laid plan to find out what his friends really thought of him.' Dr. Morelle looked towards the dining room. 'He's in there. He would, no doubt, still like to know the answer.'

June stared at him incredulously.

'You can't — mean that . . . ' She turned and went unsteadily towards the dining room. On reaching the door she called out: 'Brian! Brian . . . ' and dashed wildly into the dining room.

Dr. Morelle stood quietly looking after her for a second, then moved back to the desk.

After a few moments June reappeared in the doorway, and leaned against the doorpost. Then, glaring at Dr. Morelle, she moved moving to a chair to the left of the desk. 'You rotten . . . '

'I am trying to find a murderer,' Dr. Morelle was unmoved.

June sank into the chair. 'Oh, God!' she said brokenly.

'Half an hour ago he was shot dead in this room,' Dr. Morelle said. 'If there is anything you can tell me, that will help.'

June looked up and met his eyes. 'You want me to help? You're very clever, Dr. Morelle. You've done what I thought no power on earth could do. Made my love for Brian live again, for a moment. I hope you'll never know how much it hurt, or how deeply I hate him for having destroyed it; so deeply that even the name of his murderer is safe in my hands.'

'Miss Lister . . . ' Dr. Morelle began.

June got to her feet. 'Whoever it was only did what I'd have done, if I'd had the guts.' She faced Dr. Morelle defiantly.

Miss Frayle entered the room and stopped short. 'Oh, I'm so sorry. I thought you'd finished.'

June recovered herself with an effort. 'We have. And the net result of our little interview is the return of one earring.'

Miss Frayle came forward. 'Oh, splendid. Dr. Morelle told me he'd found it.'

'I dropped it in this room three nights ago,' June said.

'In this room?' Miss Frayle said, surprised.

'Yes, why?'

'Dr. Morelle found it in the dining room.'

At this revelation, June looked at Dr. Morelle and sank back into her chair.

Dr. Morelle tightened his lips and turned away in exasperation.

June looked up at Miss Frayle. 'What did you say?'

'He found your earrings in the dining-room,' Miss Frayle repeated.

June looked, at Dr. Morelle in embarrassment as he glared at Miss Frayle. 'You have a genius, Miss Frayle, unparalleled in my experience — '

'Oh, Doctor — ' Miss Frayle preened herself as she moved nearer the fireside.

' — for saying the wrong thing at the wrong time,' Dr. Morelle finished bitingly.

June recovered herself and looked at Dr. Morelle. 'Very well. I did lose it in the dining room.'

'When?'

'After I'd left Philip here that night with Cartwright . . . I came back.'

'Alone?' Dr. Morelle snapped.

'Yes.'

'Why?'

'As I was saying good night to the others at the gate, I noticed the dining room windows were open,' June explained. 'I suddenly thought that someone might be there, and might have overheard all that had been said.'

'So you went back to find out?' Miss Frayle asked. 'I should have been scared.'

'I was pretty scared myself.' June paused. 'You see, there was someone there.'

Miss Frayle gasped and sat down in the nearest armchair.

'Who was it?' Dr. Morelle questioned sharply.

June shrugged. 'It was dark. I couldn't see. But as I went into the room I heard someone — move. I'm afraid I didn't wait for any more. I turned and ran.'

'Miss Wells and Forbes can corroborate this?' Dr. Morelle pressed.

June hesitated. 'Evelyn can.'

'And Forbes?'

'I'd — I'd rather not say.'

'I would prefer that you did,' Dr. Morelle insisted.

June got up and began to pace. 'I tell you it's not important.'

'Well, I must say it's all perfectly clear to me,' Miss Frayle said airily. 'Mr. Cartwright was in this room with Major Troon. Miss Wells and Mr. Forbes were by the gate and — 'she indicated June — 'you were at the French windows. It's obvious the only person who could have been in that room was . . . '

'I can hardly wait to hear,' Dr. Morelle commented ironically.

' . . . Miles,' Miss Frayle finished triumphantly.

'It is a perpetual source of wonder to me, Miss Frayle, how you are always one step ahead of me,' Dr. Morelle said sarcastically.

Miss Frayle was deflated. 'But who else could it have been?'

'It would not occur to you, of course, that Miss Lister may wish us to believe it was Miles.' Dr. Morelle said suavely.

'That's not true!' June protested.

'Then why cannot Forbes confirm your story?'

'I refuse to tell you.'

Dr. Morelle shrugged. 'You leave me no option but to ask him myself.'

'Go ahead. Ask Nigel. Ask Nigel anything you like,' June snapped.

Dr. Morelle turned as Guthrie re-entered the room. 'Mr. Guthrie, would you mind?'

'Forbes?' Guthrie smiled faintly. 'You're just in time.'

'What do you mean?' June demanded.

'If you want him sober,' Guthrie said dryly, and went out again.

June gave a start and looked at Dr. Morelle anxiously. 'Dr. Morelle, if he's like that, it's a waste of time. He won't know what's he saying! Doctor, you don't understand!'

'Of what, Miss Lister, are you afraid?' Dr. Morelle said gently.

June seated herself to the right of the desk as Forbes appeared in the doorway, followed by Guthrie. It was obvious that Forbes was the worse for drink.

He looked at Dr. Morelle blearily. 'So you've got round to me at last?' he slurred, heading unsteadily towards the drinks table. 'Nigel Forbes, last in the queue, because there's nothing he really knows.' He poured himself a large drink.

'You see, Doctor, you see.' June whispered.

'Well, what do you know, Doctor?' Forbes called. 'Do you know who killed Cartwright?'

Dr. Morelle answered quietly as he reseated himself at the desk. 'Not yet.'

'Not yet.' Forbes set down the decanter,

and picked up his glass. 'Good job Brian isn't in a hurry. Tell you your trouble, Doctor, you question the wrong people. You leave the ones who could tell you things to cool their heels in the lounge,' — he held up his brimming glass — 'till they wind up like this.' He dropped heavily on to arm of the sofa.

'Nigel . . . ' June implored.

'I sent for you to answer one question,' Dr. Morelle said briskly. 'Where did you go when you walked out of this room three nights ago?'

Forbes smiled lopsidedly. 'It's a good question. So is the answer . . . I don't know.'

'You don't know!' Guthrie exclaimed.

'I could have walked straight to the car,' Forbes said slowly. 'I could have come round to the French windows and smashed them in. I could have killed Cartwright. And I — still wouldn't know.'

June jumped to her feet in protest. 'Doctor, he hasn't the least idea what he's saying.'

'I was drunk, Doctor,' Forbes slurred, as June crossed agitatedly to the door, 'out to the wide. That's why I'm your star witness.'

'Philip! Evelyn!' June called. 'Please come — '

Forbes began moving unsteadily around the sofa. 'That's right, let them come. Let them hear what Nigel's got to tell the Doctor, what his own friends wouldn't tell him all the morning after. What's been burning a little hole in his brain for three nights, till it's burned its way out.'

Troon came in, followed by Evelyn.

'Philip, you've got to stop him,' June said.

'It's too late,' Forbes murmured. He plonked his glass on the mantelpiece, and turned to face Dr. Morelle. 'I killed a man. I killed him with my car. I didn't stop.'

There was a moment's complete silence, and Evelyn slumped on to the sofa.

Guthrie looked at Troon. 'Is that true, Major?

'It was on Saturday night, on the Kingston by-pass,' Troon began, in a low voice.

'We tried to make him stop, but he

123

drove on,' Evelyn faltered. 'He didn't know what he was doing. None of us did that night. You must believe us . . . '

Forbes began moving towards the desk, slowly and deliberately. Noticing his movement, Troon said sharply: 'What are you going to do?'

'I'm going to put us all in the clear,' Forbes said thickly. Reaching the desk, he raised the telephone receiver, and looked round the room. 'Any objection?'

A moment's pause, then:

'No, Nigel . . . ' from Troon.

'No.' June stared before her.

As Forbes began dialling a number, Troon moved behind the end of the sofa and placed a hand on Evelyn's shoulder.

'I wouldn't trouble, Forbes,' Dr. Morelle said quietly. 'They know.' Forbes turned with a blank stare. 'The man who failed to stop a car on the Kingston by-pass has been identified.'

'Oh, God!' Evelyn turned away.

'How do you know?' June demanded.

Dr. Morelle stood up. 'It was in the stop press of the *Evening Mail*. Miss Lister, would you mind ringing the bell?'

June gave a start, then obeyed the instruction. 'He was driving a Rover Sixteen and he was Mr. James Crossley of 16 Manor Drive . . . '

Forbes slowly replaced the receiver. 'You mean . . . '

Everyone in the room stared at Dr. Morelle.

' . . . that it wasn't us after all,' Troon gasped.

'Oh God!' June shuddered with relief.

Evelyn looked up at Troon. 'Philip . . . it means we didn't do it,' she said brokenly. 'We didn't . . . do it . . . '

Forbes lurched to an armchair and sat down heavily.

'And it was there waiting for us to see! Staring at us the whole time in the paper . . . ' June said wonderingly, breaking off as Miles appeared in the doorway.

'You rang, sir?'

'Miles, did Mr. Cartwright take an evening paper?' Dr. Morelle asked quietly.

'Always, sir,' Miles affirmed, coming alongside the desk.

'Was it delivered to the house?'

Miles nodded. 'At seven o'clock every night, sir.'

'Did it come tonight?'

Miles hesitated. 'Well, no, sir. Oddly enough, for the first time I remember, it wasn't delivered.'

'Oh, but that isn't true!' Miss Frayle interjected.

Dr. Morelle turned to her. 'How do you know?'

Miss Frayle stood up and spread her hands. 'Because it was in the letter-box when I arrived. I saw it there.'

There was a slight pause, Miles looked at Dr. Morelle. 'Well, it's not there now, I can assure you, sir.'

Miss Frayle sat down again. From behind the desk Dr. Morelle looked quietly round the room.

'Doctor, what are you getting at?' June demanded.

'I want to know which of you removed the evening paper from the letter-box,' Dr. Morelle said levelly.

'Removed it!' Troon exclaimed.

'So that no one should see the item in the stop press.'

'You must be mad!' Forbes got to his feet with an effort. 'Which of us would want to conceal an item that cleared us?'

Dr. Morelle smiled grimly. 'The murderer.'

'Why?' Evelyn asked, puzzled.

'Because,' Dr. Morelle explained, 'it would have destroyed the motive behind which he was shielding.'

'Look here, Doctor, once and for all,' Troon got a grip on himself. 'None of us had anything to do with Cartwright's death.'

'You must know that!' June insisted.

Dr. Morelle looked round the room. 'I know that one of you killed him'

Everyone stared at him.

'You know . . . ' Evelyn faltered.

Forbes moved alongside the desk. 'Then for God's sake tell us!' he snapped. 'Stop playing this cat and mouse game.'

'There is one last link in the evidence, which I have arranged for the mouse to supply,' Dr. Morelle said enigmatically. 'Can anyone tell me the time?'

Troon looked at him curiously. 'The time? There's a clock on the mantelpiece.'

'So I observe,' Dr. Morelle followed Guthrie in looking at the clock.

June and Evelyn both glanced at their wristwatches.

'It's twenty minutes to ten,' June said.

'I make it that,' Evelyn agreed,

Looking at his own watch, Troon said, 'A little after.'

Dr. Morelle looked at Forbes. 'And you?'

'Time you explained what this means,' Forbes bristled.

Dr. Morelle smiled faintly. 'In a moment. Miss Wells, would you be good enough to lend your watch to Miles?'

Evelyn hesitated, puzzled, then gave her watch to Miles as he moved forward to take it. She looked at Dr. Morelle as he addressed her again.

'Will you now go to the switchboard and connect the telephone in the lounge to this room? Then wait in the lounge.'

Despite being deeply puzzled, Evelyn got up and went out to obey the instruction.

'What the devil's the idea?' Troon demanded.

'The idea,' Dr. Morelle answered, 'is that we are about to stage the murder of Brian Cartwright, second performance.'

'Second performance?' Miss Frayle faltered.

'In a second performance details emerge that were missed in the first. Have you ever, Major Troon, observed a conjurer repeat his trick?' Troon stared at Doctor Morelle blankly. 'The second time you know what to look for.'

June resumed her seat on the sofa. 'The only thing is, murderers don't repeat their tricks.'

'In which case there is only one thing to do,' Dr. Morelle said deliberately.

'And that is?'

'Attempt the trick yourself.'

'If you think such a fantastic idea is likely to get you anywhere,' Forbes commented, unimpressed.

'For the second performance two of the characters are inevitably re-cast,' Dr. Morelle went on calmly. 'I shall require you, Miss Frayle, to enact the role of the late Mr. Cartwright.'

Miss Frayle gave a little start. 'But he was murdered!'

'Most convincingly,' Doctor Morelle agreed. He turned to the manservant. 'I would like you, Miles, to take the part of the murderer.'

'Yes, sir, but . . . '

'Everyone will return to the lounge and take the places they occupied at nine o'clock,' Dr. Morelle instructed. 'When they have done so, you, Miles, will lock the lounge door on the inside. At sixteen minutes to ten by Miss Wells's watch you will turn out the lights. Simultaneously I will turn out the lights here. In the darkness you will find your way to the telephone on the piano and lift the receiver. You will then go to the door, unlock it, and make your way as quickly as you can to this room.'

Miles nodded, wide-eyed. 'Yes, Doctor — '

'Isn't there a risk that the murderer himself may repeat the trick?' Troon muttered, at which Miss Frayle gave a gasp of dismay.

'I am sure Miss Frayle is grateful to you for the warning,' Dr. Morelle said sardonically.

Miss Frayle faltered: 'I — I think — perhaps Major Troon's right. Perhaps we shouldn't do this; something may happen.'

Dr. Morelle brushed the protest aside with a stern look. 'Kindly take your position at the desk.' Miss Frayle nervously crossed to behind the desk. 'Would you three others join Miss Wells in the lounge? She should have the telephone connected by now. Mr. Guthrie, I shall require your help.'

Miss Frayle sat gingerly at the desk. 'Yes, but I say, Doctor . . . '

June smiled sweetly as she got up. 'Don't worry, dear. If something does happen to you, think how it's going to help the Doctor!' Miss Frayle looked after her unhappily as she went out

Troon moved to follow, then halted to look back at Forbes, who was hesitating. 'Nigel?'

Forbes got up, but instead of heading for the door he turned and faced Doctor Morelle as he stood by the desk. 'Just a word with the Doctor,' he said quietly. 'You think you know who killed Brian.

When those lights are out, there'll be nothing but a dark passage between you and the person you suspect. That the way you want it?'

'Yes,' Dr. Morelle assented.

Forbes shrugged his shoulders. 'It's all yours.' He followed Troon out.

Dr. Morelle crossed to the door and took the key out of the lock and, returning, handed it to Miles. 'The lock is broken, but I want you to take the key with you. When you go, close the door after you and turn the hall light out.'

'Yes sir.'

'When you reach the door on your way back, go through the motions of unlocking it and come into the room.'

'I understand.'

'When you're inside, turn up the lights.' Dr. Morelle paused, then added dryly: 'I hope you will see nothing to startle you.'

With an apprehensive look, Miles inclined his head and went out, closing the door. Dr. Morelle checked his watch, murmured: 'Seventeen minutes to ten.'

Miss Frayle cleared her throat. 'Dr. Morelle . . . '

Ignoring her, he addressed Guthrie. 'By the way, the reason I chose Miles is that he knows the house. He will be able to make those moves as quickly as the murderer.'

Guthrie smiled. 'He'll have to shift.'

'Dr. Morelle . . . ' Miss Frayle said anxiously.

Still ignoring her Dr. Morelle crossed and locked the dining room door. Turning, he looked at Guthrie. 'Oh, and did you check the time from the front door to the dining room windows?'

'Exactly fifteen seconds,' Guthrie answered. 'Here's the key.'

Dr. Morelle pocketed the key. 'Fifteen seconds. Now then, Miss Frayle, are you ready to be murdered?'

'I don't feel very well.'

Dr. Morelle moved behind Miss Frayle, seated at the desk. 'That's quite in keeping with the part.' He glanced at his watch. 'Half a minute.' He looked at Guthrie. 'When you turn the lights out, start counting the seconds of a minute as regularly as you can.'

'Right.' Guthrie moved to the light switch.

'Dr. Morelle . . . ' Miss Frayle said faintly.

Still Dr. Morelle ignored her. 'Count them to yourself, but call out the quarters.'

'O.K.,' Guthrie assented.

'At the full minute both of us may be wiser.'

'And. What about me?' Miss Frayle asked plaintively.

Dr. Morelle checked his watch, now holding it in his hand. 'Fifteen seconds, Stand by.' Guthrie tensed by the light switch. 'Everyone is in their places in the lounge. This is the room and Cartwright as we left them; Cartwright at his desk smoking his cigar. Would you like a cigar, Miss Frayle, to add to the realism?'

Miss Frayle shook her head. 'I feel quite sick enough.'

'Eight seconds,' Dr. Morelle counted.

'I'm beginning to know what he felt like,' Guthrie commented.

'It's horrible!' Miss Frayle gasped.

Dr. Morelle continued the countdown, 'Three . . . two . . . one!'

Guthrie snapped out the lights.

'Miles has turned out the lights in the lounge,' Dr. Morelle's voice sounded in the darkened room. 'He is making his way now to the telephone. He should be there by now . . . taking the receiver off . . . '

The telephone rang.

'Fifteen seconds,' Guthrie said.

'Cartwright answers it . . . Miss Frayle!' Dr. Morelle snapped.

'Oh, yes — I — ' Miss Frayle lifted the receiver. 'Hello! Hello!'

Dr. Morelle resumed his commentary. 'Miles is crossing the room now to the door.'

Miss Frayle spoke into the phone in her shaking hand. 'Who is that, please?'

'Miles is unlocking the door,' Dr. Morelle continued.

'Thirty seconds,' Guthrie called.

'Hello? Hello?' Miss Frayle repeated weakly.

'He is outside the lounge now,' Dr. Morelle said. 'He is coming along the hall . . . feeling his way in the dark. Getting nearer now . . . '

'Forty-five seconds,' Guthrie continued his count.

'He should be outside the door now . . . trying to unlock it . . . ' Dr. Morelle paused at thc sound of the key turning in the lock of the door. There was a creak as it opened. 'He is coming into the room now . . . He should be standing inside the door . . . Miles!'

A gasp sounded in the darkness.

'Miles!' Dr. Morelle repeated sharply.

There was a thud and the sound of a falling body. Miss Frayle screamed.

5

'Turn up the light!' Dr. Morelle shouted,
   Guthrie switched on the lights.

The body of Miles was revealed, lying
full length on the floor to the left of the
sofa.

Dr. Morelle waved his arm at Guthrie.
'Check the hall! Quickly!'

As Guthrie hurried outside to the hall,
Dr. Morelle crossed quickly to Miles's
body and bent to examine it.

'Is — is he dead?' Miss Frayle
whispered.

Miles gave a faint moan.

'Some water!' Dr. Morelle ordered.

Miss Frayle crossed quickly to the
drinks table, slopped some water into a
glass and took a gulp.

'It's not you, Miss Frayle, we're
reviving!' Dr. Morelle snapped.

'No, Doctor — ' She handed the glass
to Dr. Morelle as Miles stirred and
opened his eyes.

'Drink this.' Dr. Morelle put the glass to the manservant's lips.

'We must keep him warm, treat for shock.' Miss Frayle had recovered herself. 'I'll go and get something — '

As she hurried out she narrowly avoided colliding with Guthrie as he returned. 'No one; not a sign anywhere,' he reported.

'Help me lift him.' With Guthrie's assistance, Dr. Morelle got Miles on to the sofa,

'What's happened?' Troon appeared in the doorway.

'Why have you left the lounge?' Dr. Morelle asked.

'We heard a scream . . . ' He caught sight of the slumped Miles. 'My God!' He looked bitterly at Dr. Morelle. 'Well, I hope you're satisfied with your repeat performance. He might have been killed.'

'He was meant to be,' Dr. Morelle said enigmatically.

Guthrie came forward. 'But why? Why pick on Miles?'

Miss Frayle returned carrying a heavy overcoat, and went over to the sofa, 'I don't know whose this is, I'm sure — '

'It looks damn like mine!' Guthrie said.

'Well, it's in a good cause, Mr. Guthrie.' Miss Frayle draped it over Miles.

Dr. Morelle addressed Troon. 'Who switched the lights on in the lounge? And when?'

'I did. When we heard the scream.'

'Was everyone present?'

Troon nodded. 'Yes. I told them to stay there.' He paused. 'Well, I hope the experiment has proved helpful.'

'It's driving me crackers,' Guthrie confessed. 'Here's a chap who's been nearly slugged to death and the only persons who could have done it were in the lounge.' He indicated Troon, then added: 'And he says no one left the lounge.'

'No one.' Troon was adamant.

'That was not altogether unexpected,' Dr. Morelle commented dryly.

Guthrie stared at him blankly.

'What do you mean?' Troon demanded.

'But, Doctor . . . ' Dr. Morelle waved Miss Frayle into silence.

'You see,' he explained, 'Cartwright's

murderer never left the lounge.'

'But he must have done — ' Guthrie protested.

'Or how could he have got in here?' Miss Frayle added

'He didn't.' Dr. Morelle turned to Troon. 'That's what the experiment has just proved.'

'How?'

'A little matter of timing.' Dr. Morelle paused. 'Cartwright was murdered within the minute when the lights were out.'

Guthrie nodded. 'Granted.'

Dr. Morelle looked at him. 'When you called out 'forty-five seconds', Miles had reached the outside of this door.

Guthrie shrugged. 'Well?'

'That means that the real murderer was left with fifteen seconds in which to unlock the door, enter the room and kill Cartwright, relock the door, leaving the key on the inside, and return to his place in the lounge before the lights went up.'

'Couldn't have been done,' Guthrie said flatly.

'Humanly and logically impossible,' Troon agreed.

'Then it was impossible for the murderer,' Dr. Morelle pointed out. 'In other words, he never left the lounge.'

Everyone stared at him blankly.

'But poor Mr. Cartwright was shot through the head in this room . . . ' Miss Frayle said.

'And Miles was nearly killed inside that door,' Guthrie added.

Dr. Morelle smiled enigmatically. 'And the question is . . . ?'

'And you think you know?' Troon asked.

'I think . . . it is time Miles was helped to his room.'

Miss Frayle took the overcoat from Miles's shoulders as Troon came round the end of the sofa and helped him to his feet.

'I don't need it, thanks,' he said weakly. 'I'm all right, just want to lie down . . . '

Miss Frayle laid the overcoat on the table behind the sofa. 'Ah, that's what you think!' she said briskly. 'Now I'm going to make you a nice cup of hot sweet tea and I'm going to . . . '

Dr. Morelle interrupted: 'Miss Frayle.'

'Yes?'

'You're going to save Miles's life — by remaining here.'

Troon looked back from the doorway, to which he had supported Miles. 'You still haven't told us why he was attacked.'

'Perhaps Miles himself has a clue,' Guthrie suggested.

'Why not ask him?' Dr. Morelle said suavely.

As Troon looked at him, Miles said quietly: 'Yes . . . I know. So does the Doctor.' Fear crept into his voice. 'But I'm not going to say. I'm not going to say anything, do you hear? Anything. Please take me to my room.'

There was a silence, then Dr. Morelle shrugged. 'It's a reasonable request, Major Troon.' Troon faced Dr. Morelle for a moment, then turned and escorted Miles out of the room. Dr. Morelle moved behind the desk. 'Miss Frayle, would you ask Miss Wells to connect this telephone with the exchange? I shall be putting through a call to Scotland Yard.'

'Scotland Yard!' Guthrie exclaimed.

'You mean — ? Oh, Dr. Morelle!' Miss

Frayle's voice took on a triumphant note. 'There you are, Mr. Guthrie. Just when everything's dark to the rest of us, when we can't see the wood for the trees — ' She turned to her employer and added: 'I wish I had your mind, Doctor!'

'Exchange in that event would be robbery,' was the dry rejoinder.

Miss Frayle went on blithely: 'Mind you, there are times when I wonder whether I'm unnaturally stupid.'

'Not in the least, Miss Frayle.'

'Oh, Doctor . . . ' Miss Frayle smiled gratefully.

'Just naturally.'

At this crushing remark the smile faded from Miss Frayle's face, and she went out hurriedly, leaving the door ajar.

Guthrie went over to the drinks table. 'Well, you can put me in the same class! And don't say 'Not in the least'.' Dr. Morelle smiled thinly. 'But damn it, here have I been helping you all the evening, right in on every move and I haven't a clue.'

Dr. Morelle shrugged. 'It's a relatively simple case.'

'Clear as mud,' Guthrie said. 'I plump for the Siamese cat.' He poured out a drink. 'Seriously, Doctor, do you know?'

'I think I do.'

'Well, let's have it,' Guthrie pressed.

'I would prefer that the lounge did not 'have it'. Close the door.'

'Well?' Guthrie crossed and closed the door.

'Lassegue,' Dr. Morelle said briefly.

Guthrie wrinkled his brow, 'Lassegue . . . But that's only a name. That doesn't tell us anything. Who is Lassegue?'

'For years he had searched for the man who sent his father to the chair.'

Guthrie raised his eyebrows. 'He? You mean it's not a she?'

Dr. Morelle began moving slowly towards the fireplace. 'I use the masculine gender purely for convenience.' He smiled thinly. 'For years he had searched for Cartwright, and caught up with him at last in London. Cartwright had never seen him, so he was able to get an introduction, become friendly and enter his home without suspicion being aroused. Three nights ago Cartwright played into his hands with a threat of blackmail. He wrote Cartwright a warning letter based on the threat, and widened the area of suspicion to four persons. Do you follow?'

Guthrie nodded. 'I follow that all right.'

'Something, however, he had never expected, happened,' Dr. Morelle went on. 'Cartwright responded to the letter by asking the four persons to dinner, with a detective and a journalist thrown in . . . '

'Not forgetting Miss Frayle,' Guthrie put in dryly, seating himself on the sofa.

'Never forgetting Miss Frayle. There was to be no privacy for Lassegue. He was forced to work under bright lights and everyone's eyes. Nevertheless he brought it off. So ingeniously that although I know when, where and by whom the murder was committed, I remain in the dark as to how. And I would still be in the dark as to who, but for chance.'

'Chance?' Guthrie said sharply.

Dr. Morelle moved to the far end of the sofa and stood facing the journalist. 'Since the murder, Lassegue had made two slips; simple and natural slips, but both fatal.'

'What were they?'

'A few moments ago I inquired the time. Three persons produced watches. Lassegue did not.'

'He may not have had one,' Guthrie said quietly.

'He had one at dinner, earlier in the evening he told me the time.' Dr. Morelle paused, then added significantly: 'He did not produce his watch because it was a luminous one.'

'And the second slip?'

Dr. Morelle began moving back to the desk. 'That was less pardonable. The changing of the switchboard in the hall.'

Guthrie stood up. 'I don't follow.'

'There's only one time when it could have been done,' Dr. Morelle explained. 'When everyone had returned to the lounge after the murder.'

'Well?'

'The first person to come out of the lounge was Miss Wells, who is emphatic she never touched it and that no one went near it after her.'

Guthrie shrugged. 'She's lying.'

Dr. Morelle shook his head. 'She's

telling the truth.'

'Then it couldn't have been changed by anyone,' Guthrie said, staring.

'Logically by one person. And that person is Lassegue.'

Guthrie turned and sat on the arm of the sofa, facing the desk. 'I'm afraid I'm quite at sea.'

Dr. Morelle regarded him steadily from the front of the desk. 'Permit me to bring you into harbour. Lassegue intended to murder Cartwright three nights ago.' He pointed to the dining room. 'He was waiting in that next room to do so, when he overheard the threat of blackmail.'

Guthrie became rigid.

'That decided him to wait,' Dr. Morelle went on implacably. 'When tonight came, he was able to be present because the reason of his association with Cartwright, the nature of his employment, made his presence perfectly natural.'

Guthrie glanced towards the door. 'Miles! Of course. Well I'm damned!'

'I am afraid you are — *Mr. Lassegue!*'

Guthrie turned to find Dr. Morelle's revolver levelled at him.

Guthrie gave a short, easy laugh as he stood up. 'What the hell do you mean?'

'I mean that you killed Cartwright from the lounge. You changed the switchboard when I first sent you out of this room after the murder. You tried to kill Miles at that door, because he was meeting someone tomorrow who would identify you.'

Guthrie laughed. 'Look, Doctor, I don't know whether I'm expected to take this seriously . . . '

Dr. Morelle moved the revolver. 'You are.'

'Then I would respectfully ask what proof there is I did any one of those things?' He took out a cigarette. 'The evidence that I changed the switchboard rests on Miss Wells, who could be lying. No one saw me lay a finger on Miles!

'As for Cartwright, when he was killed I was locked in a lounge with seven other persons. You've spent the evening proving conclusively that there wasn't time for any of us to have left the lounge, committed the murder and got back again. You have, in fact, provided me with a cast-iron alibi, for which I am duly grateful.' He smiled crookedly. 'Where do we go from there, Doctor? I'm ready to be entertained.'

'You're ready, I hope,' Dr. Morelle said grimly, 'to explain how the paperweight which struck Miles travelled from the desk near which you were standing, to the floor behind the sofa.'

'Anyone could have moved it,' Guthrie scoffed. 'You yourself.'

'With your fingerprints?'

Guthrie gave a slight start.

Covering him all the time with the revolver, Dr. Morelle moved slowly towards the table behind the sofa. 'When the police check those fingerprints, they'll also check on your identity. You'll be able to explain, of course, the distinction between 'Guthrie' and 'Lassegue'. As Guthrie remained silent, Dr. Morelle went on, 'You'll be able to explain, I have no doubt, why Cartwright's evening paper found its way to your overcoat pocket!'

With a swift movement Dr. Morelle drew the paper from the overcoat on the table behind the sofa.

Guthrie was still retaining his composure. 'You know, Doctor, I can't help feeling sorry for you. You've gone to so much trouble and proved so much. And you still can't prove I killed Cartwright. The jackpot question, I believe he called it.' He paused, smiling. 'And do you know why you can't? Because you don't know *how* I did it. And until you know how, that cast-iron alibi remains.'

Dr. Morelle backed towards the fireplace. 'I shall rely on the Yard to break it.'

Still smiling, Guthrie calmly sat down in a chair to the right of the desk.

'On the Yard? Dr. Morelle go cap in hand with half a case for the police to finish? I don't think so! No, Doctor; I don't think you're ready for the police just yet.' His tone changed. 'Neither am I. They'll ask me questions. I don't like the police, or questions. I want to walk out of this house as I came in, a free man, alone.' He looked challengingly at Dr. Morelle. 'You know, I think you and I can do a deal, Doctor.'

'A deal?'

Guthrie nodded complacently. 'I'll give you the chance of finding out how I killed Cartwright.'

Dr. Morelle pondered for a moment, then: 'Most considerate. May I ask how?'

'By trying to kill you in exactly the same way.'

'Even more considerate. And should you succeed?'

Guthrie spread his hands. 'I shall be free.'

'Is that the deal?'

Guthrie shrugged. 'I may fail. If I do, it'll be because you have learned the secret . . . You'll have got your case.'

'The deal has certain attractions,' Dr. Morelle said slowly. 'Unless, of course it's a ruse to get out of this room.'

'The front door's locked,' Guthrie pointed out. 'Where would I go? There's no trick but the one I intend to play.' He glanced at his wristwatch.

'And what do I do?' Dr. Morelle asked. 'Stand here and wait for the blow?'

'There's no obligation to stand. You can sit or move about.'

'And you?' Dr. Morelle queried sharply.

Guthrie shrugged carelessly. 'You can do what you like with me. Raise my hands above my head, tie them behind my back. Put me in the lounge, if you like, under lock and key.'

'And I shall still be shot in this room?'

Guthrie rose slowly. 'As Cartwright was. By the way, there should be a time limit to any deal. You said you would phone the police. I suggest you do so at ten o'clock.'

'At ten o'clock?'

'Yes.' Guthrie looked at the other eagerly. 'Agreed?'

'There's no special point about ten o'clock,' Dr. Morelle queried. 'It could be at one minute past?'

Guthrie hesitated. 'I think it should be at ten o'clock.' He crossed the back of the sofa towards the fireplace.

Dr. Morelle smiled faintly. 'That's rather what I expected you to say.' He moved round towards the desk. 'At ten o'clock, if I lift this receiver, I shall be shot.' He paused and looked at Guthrie. 'Correct?'

Guthrie nodded. 'Through the right

temple, if you wish to be precise.'

'The right temple,' Dr. Morelle repeated thoughtfully.

'You'll be happy to know death will be instantaneous,' Guthrie assured him.

'You have taken a load off my mind,' Dr. Morelle said dryly. 'And this will happen no matter where you are, in here or in the lounge.'

Guthrie looked at his watch. 'It's four minutes to ten,' he said pointedly.

'You were in the lounge when Cartwright was killed,' Dr. Morelle mused.

'You will make that call, Doctor?' Guthrie prompted.

Dr. Morelle moved around the desk, 'Your physical presence is not essential to these crimes . . . The victim is not shot by you, but by someone or something that functions for you.'

'Come now, Doctor — '

Dr. Morelle looked about him. 'Somewhere in this room, a device timed to go off at ten precisely, trained on the telephone, set like an alarm clock. First at nine for Cartwright, then at ten for me . . . ' He looked at Guthrie. 'That was

153

daring of you, to alter it under my very nose. That is why you chose ten o'clock, exactly one hour later. *One click further on of the mechanism.*'

'You're doing well. And it's three minutes to.'

'Let's see,' Dr. Morelle glanced about, 'where have you been standing?'

Guthrie calmly seated himself on the sofa, and waved his hand. 'By the mantelpiece a good deal.'

Dr. Morelle crossed behind the sofa towards the mantelpiece. 'And what has the mantelpiece to offer us? A clock . . . but how topical since we're discussing time. In three minutes it will strike the hour. I wonder if there is anything else it will do.' He paused, watching Guthrie closely. 'Vary its normal procedure, perhaps, and fire a shot neatly directed through the winding hole in the face.' Turning the clock round, he examined it carefully before replacing it.

'I wish I'd thought of it,' Guthrie said calmly. 'But even I could not import a clock without attracting attention. Or having done so, ensure that it was trained on the telephone.' He smiled. 'And it's two minutes to.'

Dr. Morelle came behind the sofa to stand below the desk. ''Import without attracting attention',' he repeated. 'That's the key! Something small enough to go in a pocket, commonplace enough to escape attention; that could be left unnoticed, trained on the victim.' He walked round the room. 'But when trained? And how in the victim's presence?' He looked at Guthrie's mocking face. 'You must have been prepared to operate before an audience; before both Cartwright and myself.'

'Not forgetting Miss Frayle,' Guthrie smiled.

'In the simplest and most natural way . . . ' Dr. Morelle broke off and, moving towards the table behind the sofa paused at the overcoat that Miss Frayle had placed on it. 'In the simplest and most natural way. You have been very clever, Mr. Guthrie.' Their eyes met.

'It's nice to be appreciated.' Guthrie rose rather unsteadily and dropped into an armchair nearer the desk.

'You almost succeeded.' Dr. Morelle backed slowly towards the desk, his revolver levelled. 'In the presence of Cartwright and myself. You even asked permission to train it on its target.' Slowly he seated himself at the desk. 'The left hand a little more forward . . . the chin slightly up . . . ' he broke off as Miss Frayle came back into the room.

'Sorry I've been so long. I've just made a lovely cup of tea.'

Dr. Morelle looked at her. 'Miss Frayle, would you give Mr. Guthrie his overcoat?'

'Why, is he going?' Miss Frayle turned and lifted the overcoat from the table behind the sofa where she had placed it earlier. She saw an object underneath. 'Oh — a camera!' she exclaimed.

'Don't touch it!' Dr. Morelle called sharply.

'You . . . ' Guthrie started forward.

'Stay where you are!' Dr. Morelle raised the revolver, and began dialling with his other hand.

Miss Frayle screamed.

'You can't, you can't, I tell you!' Guthrie's composure snapped completely. 'He killed my father. He sent him to the chair — '

Alerted by Miss Frayle's scream, Troon and Forbes burst through the doorway, the others following.

' — I only did what any son would have done!' Guthrie sobbed.

'That will be for the court to decide,' Dr. Morelle told him, then spoke into the phone: 'Scotland Yard? This is Dr. Morelle speaking . . . ' Through the open doorway, the hall clock began striking the quarters. ' . . . from five River Drive, Chelsea.'

Guthrie shouted hysterically: 'You shan't do it! You shan't — I tell you! I won't let you . . . ' he broke off as he was suddenly seized by Troon and Forbes.

Dr. Morelle concluded his phone call to Scotland Yard. 'A man has been killed . . . in most unusual circumstances . . . '

Guthrie was struggling desperately with Troon and Forbes. 'Take your hands off me, let me go! Let me get at him, I say . . . '

With a sudden convulsive movement, Guthrie wrenched himself free and made a dash in the direction of Dr. Morelle as he vacated the seat behind the desk.

The hall clock struck the hour.

157

'For God's sake, Guthrie!' Dr. Morelle shouted a hoarse warning. 'The camera!'

As Guthrie came in a direct line between the camera and the telephone, a shot rang out.

Guthrie's body stiffened, crumpled and crashed to the floor.

Dr. Morelle stood looking down at the fallen body. 'Most unusual . . .' he murmured.

'For God's sake!' muttered June Lister.

'His camera — it was his bloody camera — ' Forbes said.

'It killed *him* — this time,' whispered Evelyn Wells.

'It's a gun all right,' commented Troon, holding up the camera, 'not his actual camera — but a replica.'

'Some easily handled, inconspicuous instrument of death,' Dr. Morelle commented, 'which could be left unnoticed, aimed at the prospective target . . .'

There was a sudden scratching at the French windows and a strange mewing cry. Miss Frayle turned sharply with a gasp. 'What — what — ?'

'It's Mr. Smith — he wants to come in.' And Miles went to let the white cat in.

ACT OF VIOLENCE

(Adapted from the radio play by Ernest Dudley)

In the courtroom of the Old Bailey there came the sound of the shuffling of feet as the Jury returned. The Clerk of the Court cleared his throat, then his voice came clearly:

'Members of the Jury, are you agreed upon your verdict?'

'We are.' The Foreman of the Jury answered.

'Do you find the prisoner, Robert Griffiths, Guilty or Not Guilty of murder?' the Clerk asked.

'Guilty.'

'You find the prisoner Guilty and that is the verdict of you all?' the Clerk pressed.

'That is our unanimous verdict,' the Foreman confirmed.

The Clerk turned to look at the accused man. 'Prisoner at the bar, you stand convicted of murder; have you anything to say why sentence of death should not be passed upon you according to law?'

An anguished expression passed over Robert Griffith's face. 'I'm innocent. I'm absolutely innocent!' he pleaded.

Above and to one side of him the Judge looked down at him, stone-faced and unmoved. 'Robert James Griffiths,' he said implacably, 'the sentence of the Court upon you is that you be taken from this place to a lawful prison and thence to a place of execution and that you be hanged by the neck until you are dead . . . '

★   ★   ★

Miss Frayle answered the telephone. 'Hello? This is Dr. Morelle's secretary.'

She listened as a Welsh voice sounded in the receiver. 'Is that Dr. Morelle's house in Conway?'

'Yes; who is that?'

'Professor Owen,' the caller answered. 'I'm speaking from Little Conway.'

'Oh, hello, Professor.' Miss Frayle recognized the caller. 'This is Miss Frayle. I'm up here with Dr. Morelle.'

'I thought he was staying at Conway for a holiday,' Owen said, puzzled.

'That was the original idea,' Miss Frayle conceded. 'Then he decided there was some work he must do, and here I am.' She added, dryly: 'It makes a change from London, anyway.'

'I was going to ask him to come over for dinner this evening,' Owen said uncertainly.

'I'm sure he'd like to,' Miss Frayle said reassuringly. 'He's working with the dictaphone at the moment, shall I get him for you?'

'I don't want to disturb him. If he can't come this evening, what about tomorrow evening?'

'Tomorrow — that's Saturday, isn't it, Professor Owen?'

'Is it? Oh, yes, so it is.'

Miss Frayle smiled. 'I think you'd better hold on, while I get the Doctor.'

'If you're sure it's not bothering him?'

'Of course not, he'd like to speak to you.' Miss Frayle laid the receiver down, and went in search of Dr. Morelle in the next room.

Dr. Morelle was murmuring into a Dictaphone: 'A certain Australian tribe buries the murdered victim's corpse and smoothes the earth round the grave. A watch is kept on the grave, and the first insect that runs over it, shows the direction in which to look for the murderer . . .' He broke off as the door opened, and his secretary entered.

'Oh, Dr. Morelle — It's Professor Owen on the 'phone for you.'

'Let me switch off the machine.'

Miss Frayle waited respectfully, then said: 'He wants to know if you can go over for dinner this evening.'

'I don't think I can.'

'Why not?' A note of reproof crept into Miss Frayle's voice. 'You're supposed to be here on holiday.'

Dr. Morelle frowned. 'I wanted to finish this work over the weekend.'

'A break will do you good,' Miss Frayle insisted. 'Besides, Professor Owen would like you to go over.'

Dr. Morelle sighed heavily. 'I'll speak to him.' He went into the adjoining room, and picked up the telephone receiver lying on the table.

'Hello, Professor? Dr. Morelle here.'

'Eh? Who's that?' the lilting, slightly reedy voice sounded in the instrument.

'Dr. Morelle.'

'Oh?'

'You wanted to speak to me?' Dr. Morelle said heavily.

'Dr. Morelle? Oh, of course, I'm so sorry. My mind was wandering, I'm afraid. I hope I haven't disturbed you?'

'What do you want?' Dr. Morelle asked patiently.

'I wondered if you would come over for dinner — this evening, or tomorrow. I'm only about ten miles from you, you know.'

Dr. Morelle hesitated. 'That's very kind of you, but — '

'Which is the best evening? I've got a lot to talk about. I've been working on a new idea, and I think it's going to succeed — '

'Congratulations. I don't quite know when I could get away, I've got some work — '

'I thought you were supposed to be on holiday,' Owen said shrewdly.

'Yes, but — '

'Then you don't have to worry about work,' Owen said firmly. 'You just come on over this evening — we'll be expecting you about six-thirty.'

'Tomorrow evening would be better.'

'It's Saturday tomorrow, and I've suddenly remembered.' Owen chuckled. 'I've got a wedding on.'

'A wedding?' Dr. Morelle was surprised.

'What's that, Doctor?' Miss Frayle came into the room. 'Someone getting married?'

Dr. Morelle put his hand over the mouthpiece. 'Quiet, Miss Frayle.'

'Oh, so sorry.'

'Got to go to it,' Owen's voice went on, 'nuisance and all that, but I'm getting married.'

'In that case it would be as well if you are present,' Dr. Morelle said dryly. 'Who is your bride-to-be, may I ask? Or have you forgotten that?'

Owen laughed. 'Miss Lloyd — you know, my secretary.'

'Oh, yes.'

'Now, what about this evening? You will come?'

'Very well,' Dr. Morelle conceded. 'You're most kind. About six-thirty.'

'And bring that young woman of yours with you, if you like. What's her name — ? Miss Frayle.'

'I am aware she would be delighted,' Dr. Morelle said heavily. 'Goodbye, Professor.'

'Goodbye, see you at six-thirty. You know how to get here?'

'I came to see you the summer before last,' Dr. Morelle reminded his caller. 'I presume you haven't moved?'

'No, I'm still here. Tomorrow evening then.'

The line clicked as Owen rang off. As he replaced the receiver, Dr. Morelle smiled faintly.

'What are you smiling at, Doctor?' Miss Frayle asked. 'The idea of someone getting married?'

'Professor Owen really is the popular conception of an absent minded professor.'

Miss Frayle pouted. 'He sounded

167

rather nice. As if he might be quite attractive in a kind of way.'

'What kind of way, Miss Frayle?'

'Well, you know — '

'I'm afraid I don't,' Dr. Morelle shrugged. 'However,' he added dryly, 'I am sure his secretary does.'

'What do you mean?'

Dr. Morelle smiled at his secretary's comical expression. 'They are to be married tomorrow.'

'How wonderful!'

'It will be if he remembers to be there.'

Miss Frayle looked thoughtful. 'Professor Owen's secretary, is she awfully attractive?'

'I can't recall.'

'I suppose you wouldn't,' Miss Frayle sighed.

'Anyway,' Dr. Morelle shrugged, 'I'm surprised that he ever noticed if she was.'

'Well, he has, Dr. Morelle, hasn't he?' Miss Frayle tightened her lips. 'And better late than never.'

'You sound a trifle tense, Miss Frayle,' Dr. Morelle said suavely. 'Is anything the matter?'

'Nothing at all, Doctor, nothing at all.'

'For a moment, I was beginning to wonder if — '

'What?'

'Nothing at all, Miss Frayle, nothing at all, Professor Owen has invited you as well.'

Miss Frayle recovered her composure. 'How very kind of him. It will be nice to meet him and his secretary.' She hesitated, then added thoughtfully: 'Professor Owen has an assistant, hasn't he?'

'Yes.'

'I saw him in Conway the other day, and you told me who he was, Glyn — Glyn something-or-other.'

'Evans, his name is.'

'A dark, good-looking young man. He was with a tall, attractive young woman. Perhaps she was Professor Owen's secretary?

'Perhaps.'

'If it was, I rather thought he had his eye on her,' Miss Frayle said darkly.

'Professor Owen is the much more brilliant brain.'

Miss Frayle gave him an indignant

169

look. 'And you think that's why she fell in love with him? Because he's cleverer?'

Dr. Morelle sighed heavily. 'My dear Miss Frayle, I have no intention of entering into a discussion with you on the subject of what attracts one female member of the human species to a male, and vice-versa.'

'Oh, but why not?'

Dr. Morelle turned away actively. 'Because I have more important matters to attend to.'

Miss Frayle looked after his departing figure and sighed to herself. 'Oh dear, just for a moment I thought I'd got him going!'

★　★　★

As Professor Owen put down the telephone, his fiancée came into the room. Mary Lloyd was a tall, svelte woman in her late twenties, with widely spaced brown eyes. 'Who were you telephoning, David?'

'Oh, hello, Mary. I've been talking to Dr. Morelle.'

'Did you mention that you and I are to be married tomorrow?'

'Mention it to who, my dear?'

'Dr. Morelle of course. Haven't you just been speaking to him on the phone?'

'Yes, yes. I told you. Er — I did mention about our getting married tomorrow.'

The girl came forward and rested her hands on his shoulders, looking directly into his eyes. 'David, I suppose you are going through with it, aren't you?'

Owen smiled faintly. 'I'm afraid you're overworked, Mary. We've been going at the job non-stop several months.'

'You haven't answered my question,' the girl reproved.

'It hardly requires an answer. You know that I'm marrying you tomorrow.'

Mary gently disengaged her hands. 'I don't think I could take it if you let me down.'

Owen frowned. What are you talking about? Whatever put the idea in your head — ?'

'Mary . . . ' A male voice sounded faintly outside the room, through the half-open door.

'Quiet,' Owen whispered, 'here's Glyn.'

'There you are, Mary. Hello, David.' Glyn Evans pushed the door further open, and entered the room. He was a good foot taller than the older man, with thick dark hair, carefully combed, contrasting sharply with Owen's own thinning, sandy hair.

'Are you just going? Owen asked him.

'Yes, I'll be back this evening, after rehearsal.'

Mary laughed lightly. 'You and your amateur theatricals.'

Evans gave a self-deprecatory smile. 'I know — just a stage-struck fool.'

'Dr. Morelle is coming over for dinner,' Owen informed him.

'Is he?' Evans spoke casually. 'I saw him in Conway the other day.'

'With Miss Frayle,' Mary added.

'So try and get back before they go,' Owen invited. 'Miss Frayle is coming too.'

Evans nodded. 'I'd like to meet them. You and Mary are working this afternoon?'

'Just one or two odds and ends,' Owen confirmed.

Evans spread his hands. 'I don't know why you're rushing it this way.'

'David must have it all cleared up before the wedding,' Mary defended.

'Why not postpone it?'

'Thank you. I'm sure,' Mary said tightly.

Owen frowned. 'Not all of your jokes are in the best taste, Glyn.'

'I'm sorry,' Evans smiled contritely

'I'm going to the laboratory,' Owen said.

'See you tonight — I'll get back soon as I can after rehearsals,' Evans promised. 'So long, David.'

'Goodbye.' Owen moved to the door and glanced back at his fiancée. 'Come along, Mary.'

Mary hesitated. 'Just coming,' she called after him. She looked at the smiling Evans. 'I hope you enjoy your play-acting.'

Evans raised an eyebrow. 'Now whose making jokes in bad taste?'

Mary frowned slightly. 'I don't know what you mean. I was referring to these amateur theatricals you're so mad about.'

'You know that I'm play-acting all the

time I'm with you and David, so that he won't suspect I'm in love with you.'

'Please don't talk like that,' Mary snapped.

'For the last time, won't you listen to me?' Evans implored.

'There's your arrogance again,' Mary said. 'Just because you're in love with me, or say you are — '

'You know I love you more than anything in the world.'

'And so I have to love you,' Mary said scornfully. 'You can't believe that I should turn you down for David.'

'I know he's got the money,' Evans said cynically. 'He can give you security.'

Mary tightened her lips. 'I think perhaps we'd better not discuss it any more.'

'There's some motive for what you're doing,' Evans said thoughtfully. 'Why don't you confide in me?'

'How dare you talk to me in this horrible way!' Mary flared.

Evans shrugged. 'Put on your airs if you like, but it doesn't fool me. I know you don't really love him. You really love me.'

'You conceited fool!'

Evans frowned. 'I don't like being called that.'

'And I don't like having to listen to any more of your rubbish.'

'Mary, come along.' Owen's distant voice was impatient.

'Just coming, David,' Mary called. 'We'll see you this evening,' she told Evans coldly.

'All right. And I still say you're in love with me and not him.'

★   ★   ★

'What a lonely road, Dr. Morelle,' Miss Frayle commented from the front passenger seat of Dr. Morelle's speeding Duesenberg. She glanced through the side window and added: 'Even though the view across the estuary is very lovely.'

At the wheel, Dr. Morelle was staring ahead with a slight frown. 'At the moment I am more concerned with the road to Little Conway.' He began to apply the breaks.

'I know this short cut will get us there

in half the time,' Miss Frayle said confidently. 'Why are you slowing the car?'

'While I may be following the direction you gave me, Miss Frayle — '

'I was only reading what it says on this map,' Miss Frayle defended herself, holding up the folded map resting on her knees.

'I am not certain that you are reading from the *right* map,' Dr. Morelle said heavily.

Miss Frayle gave a long sigh.

Dr. Morelle shot her a sideways glance. 'What was it, Miss Frayle, that made you sigh so profoundly?'

'It must be marvellous always to feel so sure you're right, and the other person must be wrong.'

'I merely recall that the road I took before to Little Conway was less devious than this,' Dr. Morelle said mildly.

Miss Frayle was looking up the road. 'There's a garage ahead, how about asking there?'

'A sensible suggestion,' Dr. Morelle agreed.

They moved on until the garage was reached, and then Dr. Morelle stopped the car. There was a small office next to the petrol pump, with a banner proclaiming 'Robert Griffiths (Prop.).'

As a figure in overalls came out and approached the car, Miss Frayle said: 'I'll ask this man.' Before he could inquire what they wanted she added: 'Are we right for Little Conway please?'

'Little Conway?' the man said. He was tow-haired, with serious blue eyes. As she appraised him, Miss Frayle guessed his age at around thirty. 'You're going the long way round — ' he broke off abruptly, his expression changing.

'What's the matter?' Miss Frayle asked, surprised.

'I — that is — '

'I somehow thought there was a shorter route,' Dr. Morelle said smoothly.

The man recovered his composure. 'That's right — yes, sir,' he said slowly. 'Take the second turning on the right, that'll get you back to the right road.'

'Oh, dear. Thank you,' Miss Frayle realized that Dr. Morelle had been right

— as usual. 'I'm sorry to have bothered you.'

'Anywhere particular you want in Little Conway?' the man asked.

'Professor Owen's house, perhaps you know it?' Miss Frayle asked hopefully.

'I know it,' the man nodded. 'You'd have gone miles out of your way; this other road, you can't miss it.'

'Thank you,' Miss Frayle said.

As Dr. Morelle switched on the engine the man said, 'Good evening, Miss. Good evening — er — Doctor.'

As they drove away, Miss Frayle looked at Dr. Morelle and frowned. 'That was funny, wasn't it?'

Dr. Morelle remained expressionless. 'What, my dear Miss Frayle?'

'That young man. The sudden look on his face — ' Miss Frayle faltered, then added wonderingly, ' — as if he'd seen a ghost.'

'I wasn't noticing particularly.'

'Of course you were, 'Miss Frayle said firmly. 'I believe it was something to do with you.'

Dr. Morelle raised an eyebrow. 'What

aroused that dark suspicion in your mind?'

'The way he acted.' A sudden gleam entered Miss Frayle's eyes. 'I've just thought of something.'

'What, again?' Dr. Morelle said dryly.

'How did he know you were a doctor? He said, 'Good evening, doctor'.'

'I can answer that without much difficulty. He heard you call me Dr. Morelle.'

Miss Frayle pouted. 'Oh, did I? That explains it . . . ' she broke off as a turning became visible ahead. 'Oh dear, d'you know, I've forgotten whether he said second or third turning.'

'I haven't.' Dr. Morelle slowed and took the next turning.

'There are more houses coming up now, Doctor,' Miss Frayle said, her propensity for stating the obvious as well to the fore as ever. 'We shall soon be there.'

'I recollect the road now,' Dr. Morelle murmured. 'There's a level crossing ahead.'

He slowed the car as they approached the closed gates, then stopped as the whistling of a train sounded.

'Isn't it fascinating to watch?' Miss Frayle commented, as the train rattled past.

'It has a charm all of its own,' Dr. Morelle said ambiguously.

'There's a signpost,' Miss Frayle said. She read aloud: 'Little Conway: half a mile.'

'Thank you, Miss Frayle,' Dr. Morelle said heavily.

'Oh, do you see that poster — a concert at the village hall. What fun . . . and look, Doctor. Robert Griffiths is performing.'

'So I observed. The young man at the garage.' Dr. Morelle released the hand-brake and the car moved forward as the gates opened again.

'That's what I was thinking, but I'm surprised at you, though,' Miss Frayle smiled.

'Indeed?'

'Just because that's the name of the garage, doesn't mean it's his name,' Miss Frayle explained. 'He could be an employee there,' she finished, pleased with her little flight of logic.

'I am gratified that the holiday hasn't dulled your sharp wits,' Dr. Morelle commented dryly.

'Holiday? I like that,' Miss Frayle sniffed, then added condescendingly: 'I expect you're a little over-tired driving.'

'It so happens that I was already aware of his name.'

'Oh . . . ' Miss Frayle rallied after the polite put-down: 'So I was right then, he *did* recognize you.'

'I'm only surprised that he hasn't changed it.'

'What do you mean, Dr. Morelle? Where was it you'd seen him?'

'In the dock at the Old Bailey.'

★   ★   ★

Dr. Morelle slowed the car as they reached the country house of Professor Owen, with its impressively large garden.

'It's lovely, doctor!' Miss Frayle exclaimed.

'I am glad you are impressed. That's Professor Owen coming down the drive.' Dr. Morelle stopped the car.

'Hello Dr. Morelle. So glad you could

come over,' Owen smiled.

'Hello, Professor Owen.' Dr. Morelle got out of the car, and opened the door for Miss Frayle.

'And how nice to see you, Miss Frayle,' Owen said gallantly.

'How are you, Professor?' Miss Frayle closed the car door behind her.

'Come on in Miss Frayle . . . Doctor. I want you both to meet Mary — we're getting married tomorrow, you know.'

'So you said,' Dr. Morelle murmured.

'Secretary marries her boss kind of thing,' Owen smiled.

'How wonderful!' Miss Frayle exclaimed.

'Wonderful for me, anyway,' Owen said, as he approached the doorstep. 'Here we are.'

'What a nice house,' Miss Frayle commented, her eyes wide.

A tall, attractive woman appeared in the doorway. She smiled and stood aside as the party came into the house.

'Mary, Here's Dr. Morelle and Miss Frayle.'

There were handshakes as the introductions were effected

'My congratulations,' Dr. Morelle murmured.

'Thank you, Dr. Morelle,' Mary smiled.

'You're being married tomorrow, aren't you thrilled?' Miss Frayle gushed.

'Very.'

'Secretary marries her boss idea, eh?' Owen repeated.

Mary frowned slightly. 'You keep on about that, David; it happens every day.'

'Oh, does it?' Miss Frayle's eyes widened.

'You'll find out,' Mary said quietly.

'I don't think so,' Miss Frayle sighed.

Owen indicated a doorway inside. 'Come into this room, it overlooks the garden.'

'It is a pleasant view, I remember,' Dr. Morelle said, as they passed into the room.

There were two armchairs either side of a bay window, and in the centre of the room stood a table with chairs. On one side of the room stood a large glass-fronted bookcase, and a drinks cabinet and display bureau on the other.

'What wonderful big windows,' Miss

Frayle commented.

'I enjoy sitting here in the evening,' Owen smiled.

Dr. Morelle glanced at Owen's fiancée. 'Will you be staying on here?'

'Oh, yes,' Mary said promptly. 'It's ideal for David's work. He has a first-rate laboratory.'

'Not bad,' Owen agreed genially. 'Now, what are you having to drink? Miss Frayle?'

'Sherry, please.'

'Dr. Morelle?'

'I'll have some whiskey.'

'It really is a wonderful spot,' Miss Frayle enthused. 'How long have you been here?'

'I have rooms in Little Conway,' Mary replied, 'but David's been here ten years, ever since he retired from the hurly-burly of London. I've been with him all the time.'

'Yes, I've been working away, quietly, but getting quite a bit done,' Owen said modestly, handing out the drinks.

Dr. Morelle nodded as he took his glass. 'I am sure you have, Professor.' He was well aware of his scientific eminence.

Miss Frayle sipped her sherry. 'Aren't you looking forward to coming here to live, Miss Lloyd?'

'Yes, I am,' Mary affirmed. 'It is an attractive house. I move in when we come back from the honeymoon.'

'I hope you'll be able to stay and meet my assistant, Glyn Evans,' Owen said. 'He'll be looking in after rehearsals.'

'His amateur dramatics,' Mary explained. 'There's a village concert shortly.'

'We saw a poster about that on our way here, didn't we Dr. Morelle?'

'I recall noticing something about it,' Dr. Morelle admitted.

'Of course you did,' Miss Frayle said emphatically. 'That young man at the garage, Robert Griffiths, is also appearing.'

'Robert Griffiths?' Mary repeated sharply.

'Do you know him?' Miss Frayle asked.

'Who's that, Mary?' Owen looked at his fiancée.

'Griffiths,' she said briefly.

'Oh.'

'Robert Griffiths?' Dr. Morelle prompted.
Owen waved a hand dismissively. 'He

worked for me a couple of years ago. Drove my car and sort of handyman. It wasn't very satisfactory.' He lifted his glass, changing the subject. 'Cheerio, Dr. Morelle . . . Miss Frayle.'

'Your very good health, both; and a long and happy marriage,' Dr. Morelle proposed a toast.

'Yes, lots of happiness to you, Professor and Miss Lloyd,' Miss Frayle added, taking a sip of her sherry.

'Thank you,' Mary responded. 'And to your happy day — one day.' She paused, then went on: 'Do you know Robert — er — Griffiths then?'

'Dr. Morelle lost his way — ' Miss Frayle began.

'Really, Miss Frayle — '

Miss Frayle continued: 'Well you did, you tried to say it was my fault . . . Anyway, we stopped at this garage to ask, and he put us on the right road.'

'So he's running a garage, is he?' Owen muttered.

'You knew that some time ago,' Mary reminded him.

'Oh, did I? I'd forgotten.'

'I thought he was rather nice,' Miss Frayle said ingenuously. 'Good-looking, rather.'

'That was the trouble.' Owen said briefly.

'Anyway, it's all forgotten now,' Mary said hastily.

'I wonder?' Owen said slowly,

'How d'you mean, David?' Mary glanced at him sharply.

'Oh, nothing, my dear. Only he never struck me as the type who'd forget very easily.'

Mary shrugged. 'I'm sure you're wrong about him. But we mustn't bore Dr. Morelle and Miss Frayle with all this frustrated romance nonsense.'

'I'm never bored hearing about romance, frustrated or otherwise,' Miss Frayle smiled.

'Would you like to walk round the garden, Miss Frayle?' Mary said, evidently wishing to change the subject.

'I'd love to,'

As the two women went out, Owen looked at Doctor Morelle. 'Can I get you some more scotch, Doctor?'

'I'm all right, for the moment thank

you.' There was a thoughtful look in Dr. Morelle's eyes.

The two women went outside. They stood on a narrow paved path, which wound its way circuitously around the large garden. The only sounds were the low twittering of birds from the arbor.

'It's all so quiet and peaceful after London,' Miss Frayle commented.

'You work in Harley Street, don't you?'

'Yes; Dr. Morelle came up here for a holiday really. Then he started work on this criminological book — and, of course, found he couldn't get on without me.'

Mary smiled faintly. 'Quite. What's it like, being secretary to such a brilliant man?'

'Oh, he gets on with me all right,' Miss Frayle said vaguely.

'I think he's very attractive,' Mary laughed, 'in that aloof, rather chilly way.'

'Yes. He *is* a bit cold-blooded. Nothing ever surprises him. Like meeting that man at the garage.'

'Robert? What was surprising about that — oh, you mean, Dr. Morelle had met him before.'

'Er — yes.'

'In London?'

Miss Frayle hesitated. 'I — er — I think so.'

'He never talked to me about London,' Mary mused.

'Oh, didn't he?'

'It was all very difficult,' Mary admitted quietly. 'You see, he was in love with me.' Miss Frayle's eyes widened, and Mary hurried on: 'But I didn't feel that way about him. He was very nice, and it wasn't as if he was an ordinary chauffeur.'

'No?' Miss Frayle encouraged.

'But there was something I didn't take to, I could never pin it down exactly.'

Miss Frayle nodded. 'I think I understand.

Mary gave her a surprised look. 'You sound as if you know him quite well yourself.'

'Not at all,' Miss Frayle said hastily. 'I — er — I just meant that there are people that you feel odd about for no definite reason.'

Mary gave a start. 'Goodness me — I

must go and see about the eats. Our daily help also cooks for special occasions — I ought to make sure everything's all right.'

'I can continue my stroll for a bit, and then return to the house myself,' Miss Frayle offered.

'Would you mind?'

'Of course not.'

Miss Frayle looked at the woman's tall, retreating figure as she hurried back into the house. 'She's nice,' she thought to herself. 'Extraordinary meeting that young man like that. I wish Dr. Morelle hadn't shut up like an oyster about it. He really can be very irritating some-times — ' she suddenly broke off as she heard a noise coming from the arbor. Aloud, she called: 'Is that someone there?' She took a few steps towards the direction of the sound. 'Dr. Morelle?'

Robert Griffiths came out of some bushes. 'I want to speak to you,' he said quietly.

'You're the man from the garage — Robert Griffiths,' Miss Frayle said tightly.

'And you are with Dr. Morelle. You've

got to tell me something.'

'What — ?' Miss Frayle stammered uncertainly.

'Better to do what I say for Dr. Morelle's sake.'

Miss Frayle rallied. 'We're near the house; if you try anything I'll scream my head off!'

'So you know who I am. You know I'm Robert Griffiths.'

'Suppose you are?'

'And Dr. Morelle recognized me, just as I recognized him.'

'He did know your face, yes,' Miss Frayle admitted slowly.

'And what's he doing snooping down here after me?' Griffiths demanded. 'Why can't he let sleeping dogs lie?'

'What on earth are you talking about? Unless you've something to tell me — '

'I've got something to tell him all right. So you let him know I'm here.'

'Dr. Morelle? He's here with Professor Owen.'

'Better do as I say, or it'll be the worst for him,' Griffiths warned. 'Tell him I want to see him — *now*.'

'Well, I — ' Miss Frayle began hesitantly.

'Do as I say, or else,' Griffiths said grimly. 'Go and find him. I'll wait here.'

'Oh, all right.' Miss Frayle agreed. 'But I don't promise he'll come.'

Miss Frayle hurried back into the house, and found Dr. Morelle seated in one of the armchairs at the bay window. He was alone in the room.

'So there you are, Miss Frayle,' he murmured.

'Where's Professor Owen?' Miss Frayle asked.

'He's gone to find some cigars for after dinner. I think he'll remember to come back.'

'That man Griffiths wants to see you,' Miss Frayle said excitedly. 'The young man from the garage — '

'I know, I know. What's he doing here?'

'He's in the garden. He insists on seeing you. He thinks you're down here snooping after him!'

Dr. Morelle frowned. 'Unfortunate that we should have encountered each other on the way.'

'He seems in a bit of state about you.'

Dr. Morelle shrugged. 'Perhaps I should have a word with him.'

'Supposing he's got a gun or a knife?' Miss Frayle suggested worriedly.

Dr. Morelle smiled faintly. 'I don't think you need have any fears for my safety.'

'But you said he'd been tried at the Old Bailey,' Miss Frayle objected.

'He was charged with murder — '

'Murder?' Miss Frayle gave a start, and wrinkled her brows. 'Of course, I remember now. Robert Griffiths — he was found guilty of strangling that girl.'

'And ultimately his innocence was established,' Dr. Morelle pointed out.

'Yes, but it was very black against him,' Miss Frayle recalled.

'It is not the first time that a case of apparent guilt has proved to be otherwise.' Dr. Morelle got to her feet.

'If you're sure you'll be all right?'

'I'll go and speak to him,' Dr. Morelle said decisively.

★   ★   ★

It was several minutes later. Dr. Morelle was conversing with Griffiths in the arbor of Dr. Owen's garden.

'And so that's what I did, Dr. Morelle,' Griffiths was explaining. 'I decided to come back to this part of the world — I was born the other side of Caernarvon. I did think of changing my name, only changing your name isn't so easy. Anyway, Griffiths is a common enough name round here. I got a job with Professor Owen — and then — well — I left and I had the chance of this garage-business. Nobody twigged me. But now you have to come down here.'

Dr. Morelle regarded him steadily. 'What induces you to imagine I have any interest in you?'

'You were at the Old Bailey, when I was convicted. When they tried to make out I'd killed that girl.' Griffiths paused, and added bitterly: 'I might have swung for it.'

'When they realized the flaw in their case, the prosecution, as much as your own lawyers, were responsible for establishing your innocence,' Dr. Morelle pointed out. 'It may interest you to know that I added my advice to those who believed someone other than yourself was the murderer.'

Griffith frowned. 'Then what are you doing here, you're not going to tell me it's a coincidence?'

'Coincidence has a long arm. My presence here has nothing whatever to do with you,' Dr. Morelle assured the other.

'You expect me to believe that?'

'If you want my opinion, it is that you suffer from a common delusion that you have a peculiar interest for other people,' Dr. Morelle said acidly.

'If people here knew I'd been had up for murder, innocent or not, they wouldn't touch me with a bargepole,' Griffiths said angrily.

'Why should people know? It is up to you to rebuild your life. Take my advice, Griffiths, and forget that you ever were a nine days' notoriety.'

'That's what I am trying to do,' Griffiths muttered.

'Give yourself time,' Dr. Morelle advised. He turned to go, then looked back at the tense young man. 'You are young, you have plenty of time. Good evening, Griffiths.'

★ ★ ★

'That was a lovely dinner, Professor Owen,' Miss Frayle enthused, sitting back in her chair and dabbing at her lips with a serviette.

'I'm so glad,' Owen smiled.

'Mrs. Parry isn't at all a bad cook,' Mary said.

'I think she's a treasure,' Miss Frayle commented.

'How does your cigar agree with you, Dr. Morelle?' Owen asked.

'Excellently thank you, Professor.'

'They've got a most luxurious aroma,' Miss Frayle smiled.

'Will you have some more coffee, Miss Frayle?' Mary asked.

'No, thank you.'

'I sometimes think of it as a commentary upon human existence, a cigar's aroma is more exciting than the actual flavour on the palate,' Owen said reflectively.

'The shadow that proves to be more

196

alluring than the substance?' Dr. Morelle suggested.

'I think it's the same about the smell of coffee,' Mary commented, 'it's nicer than the taste.'

'Surely what we are discussing is the gulf between anticipation and realization?' Dr. Morelle stated. 'Another example is the prisoner's dream of freedom. Often after he has been freed, he will look back on his cell rather as a place of refuge against the troubles of the world which naturally beset him beyond the prison walls.'

'I suppose that's why you get unhappy love affairs,' Miss Frayle said blithely.

Dr. Morelle frowned. 'I fail to see the comparison?'

'I mean while the girl is trying to get her man,' Miss Frayle explained, 'she's thinking how wonderful it will be when she's got him, and when she has, she wonders if the trouble was really worth it.'

'And vice-versa, Miss Frayle,' Dr. Morelle pointed out.

In the ensuing pause, the sound of a car engine outside was heard.

As it stopped, Mary said: 'That sounds like Glyn's car.'

'My assistant I was telling you about, Dr. Morelle,' Owen said.

'Who's so keen on amateur theatricals,' Miss Frayle added.

They heard the sound of the front door opening and closing.

Owen glanced at Miss Frayle. 'Yes. He's usually later than this at rehearsals. But I told him you and Dr. Morelle were coming over.'

Mary got up. 'I'll go and tell him.' She opened the door and called out: 'Glyn, we're having coffee. Dr. Morelle and Miss Frayle are here.'

'Okay.' Evans responded, hanging up his coat on the stand in the hall.

Mary came back and resumed her seat. A few seconds later Evans followed her into the room.

'Ah, there you are Glyn,' Owen greeted.

'We didn't expect you so soon,' Mary said.

Evans smiled. 'You told me the great Dr. Morelle would be here — and Miss Frayle, of course.'

Owen effected introductions all round, then asked: 'What would you like, Glyn? Coffee?'

'Or a drink?' Mary suggested, pulling out another chair.

Evans seated himself at the end of the table. 'I'd have got here before — only a rather odd thing happened — I could do with a nice scotch, David.'

'I'll get it,' Mary offered.

'This is a great pleasure, Dr. Morelle, meeting you,' Evans commented. 'How are you and Miss Frayle enjoying your holiday?'

'More work than holiday for Dr. Morelle,' Miss Frayle laughed.

Dr. Morelle shrugged. 'Things have to be done. This is a most agreeable part in which to do them.'

'I love it here,' Miss Frayle said.

'I like it, too,' Evans agreed.

'Glyn is the hub around which Little Conway's social life spins,' Owen averred.

Evans gave a deprecatory smile. 'I'm keen on the amateur dramatic society, that's all.'

Mary returned with a glass of whiskey.

'Your drink, Glyn.'

'Thanks.'

'Cigar?' Owen offered a box across the table.

'Thanks, David.' Evans produced a box of matches and lighted the cigar. He blew a little cloud of smoke and resumed talking. 'The local theatrical lot were pretty dead-and-alive when I came here, as a matter of fact.'

'You've got a concert very soon, haven't you?' Miss Frayle said brightly. 'We saw a poster on our way down.'

Evans nodded. 'This coming Monday night. Star-studded entertainment. Pity you can't come to it.'

Miss Frayle pursed her lips. 'What a shame, I'd love to.'

'Why don't you come over?' Mary suggested.

Miss Frayle smiled and nodded. 'Why not?'

Evans carefully placed his cigar in an ashtray and looked across the table. 'By the way, David, I haven't told you, have I? Now this'll interest you. Dr. Morelle.'

The doctor raised an eyebrow. 'Indeed?

Something nasty in the wood shed?'

'By this morning's post — a dramatic sketch for the show, sent to our secretary — anonymously with a ten pound note towards the church funds, if we'll perform it.'

Miss Frayle wrinkled her brow. 'What an odd idea.'

'The money will come in handy, anyway,' Owen said.

'The author didn't give his name at all?' Mary asked.

Evans spread his hands. 'Not a clue.'

'It is a bit strange,' Owen mused.

Evans looked at Dr. Morelle, who had yet to comment. 'But it's a rattling good little thriller, just your cup of tea, Doctor.'

'It sounds most intriguing,' Dr. Morelle admitted.

'The secretary had it typed out — only two characters — and gave it to our two star performers to study. Rehearsals tomorrow night. Tell you what, Dr. Morelle, you ought to come to the rehearsal. Give us your expert opinion.'

'Who've you got playing the two parts?' Owen asked.

'Oh, a girl — what's her name — and that chap at the garage.'

'Who?' Miss Frayle asked sharply.

'Robert Griffiths.'

Miss Frayle looked eagerly at her employer. 'Don't you think we should see it, Dr. Morelle?'

'I can't say that amateur theatricals interest me particularly.'

'But, Dr. Morelle — '

'Quite agree with you,' Owen said gruffly. 'Bore me to death.'

'You're not being asked, David,' Mary admonished him.

Owen laughed. 'No; anyway I'm doing something tomorrow.'

'That's right, we're getting married,' Mary said briefly.

'I knew there was something,' Owen smiled.

'Pity, Dr. Morelle,' Evans said. 'Might have amused you.'

'I'm sure it would be very thrilling,' Miss Frayle prompted.

Evans looked at Dr. Morelle thoughtfully. 'Odd thing, don't you think, this anonymous business?'

Dr. Morelle shrugged slightly. 'It is not uncommon, particularly amongst a small community.'

'Like poison pen letters, you mean?' Evans suggested.

Dr. Morelle nodded. 'A similar subconscious compulsion might be responsible.'

'Poison pen letters are horrible.' Miss Frayle gave a little shudder,

'Perhaps it was you who wrote this thriller, David,' Evans said, smiling. 'Hiding your light under a bushel.'

'I fear I don't possess quite that sort of talent,' Owen said, stubbing out his cigar.

'I don't know,' Evans pursued, 'you do a lot of scribbling.'

'I hardly think you would find it had any entertainment value,' Owen replied stiffly.

'Though I'm sure it's very useful in another way,' Miss Frayle said quickly.

'Thank you, Miss Frayle,' Owen smiled.

Evans seemed determined to provoke more reaction from Dr. Morelle, who sat calmly finishing his cigar.

'Why should he send it anonymously when he's so anxious to have it done?

Hence the ten pounds bribe, so to speak.'

'Perhaps it isn't a man, perhaps it's a woman,' Mary put in.

'I fancy Mr. Evans is right in assuming the author is male,' Dr. Morelle said deliberately, stubbing out his cigar.

'What makes you say that?' Owen asked, interested.

Dr. Morelle sat back in his chair. 'Whatever imponderables may lie in the recesses of the feminine mind, one thing is certain, a woman would never go to the trouble deliberately to hide herself from the benefit of the ensuing publicity.'

'Oh, Dr. Morelle — ' Mary began.

'Not long ago there was a book by an anonymous author who turned out to be a woman,' Miss Frayle asserted. 'I forget her name, but — '

Dr. Morelle gave his sardonic smile. 'You have proved my point, Miss Frayle. If she was anonymous, how was she revealed to be a woman?'

'Pretty smart of you, Dr. Morelle,' Mary admitted.

'I agree it seems much more likely it's a man,' Evans said thoughtfully. 'But what would be his motive?'

'It might be an attempt to fix attention upon himself,' Dr. Morelle answered. 'Paradoxically, the author might feel impelled on the one hand to reveal to the world at large some innermost knowledge he possesses, while on the other to stand back in the shadows and observe the effect of his action.'

Evans digested this theory, then shrugged: 'Anyway, it's a pity you can't drive over and see us rehearsing tomorrow night.'

'Couldn't we, Doctor?' Miss Frayle implored.

'Why don't you look in just to run your professional eye over this little thriller of ours?' Evans pressed.

'Yes, we could do that,' Miss Frayle agreed eagerly.

Dr. Morelle shrugged. 'Very well, Miss Frayle, if it will interest you.'

Evans smiled broadly. 'Really, most kind of you. It'll give us a big kick, to have the great criminologist watching us.'

'Are you acting in it yourself?' Miss Frayle asked.

Evans shook his head. 'No, I'm kept

busy behind the scenes. Seeing to the props and the rest of it. It's only a short sketch but it certainly packs a punch.'

At that moment there came the sound of the telephone ringing in the hall.

Mary glanced at her fiancée. 'Shall I take it?'

Owen rose. 'No, it's all right, Mary. I'll go — though I don't know who it might be.'

'That's settled then,' Evans announced, looking at Dr. Morelle. 'You and Miss Frayle will be there? Six o'clock.'

'All right,' Miss Frayle assented.

'We'll get to the dramatic sketch about that time,' Evans explained.

Owen came back into the room. 'It's for you, Dr. Morelle,' he announced.

'For you, Doctor?' Miss Frayle glanced at him in surprise as he stood up.

'So it seems.'

'But you don't look at all surprised,' Miss Frayle said, puzzled.

Dr. Morelle raised his eyebrows. 'Should I?'

'How does anyone know you're here?' Miss Frayle said wonderingly.

'Someone does. If you'll excuse me.'

As he stepped out Miss Frayle glanced at Evans. 'I hope it doesn't mean we'll be called back to London.'

'So do I,' he agreed. 'Bit of a let-down if you can't come to our show, after all.'

In the hall, Dr. Morelle picked up the receiver where it lay beside the telephone.

'Dr. Morelle speaking.'

'It's Griffiths, Dr. Morelle,' came the caller's voice. 'Robert Griffiths.'

'Oh, yes?

'Dr. Morelle, I've got to see you.'

'Really, I can't imagine that it can be necessary. I've already reassured you about — '

'This is something that's happened since I saw you,' Griffiths interrupted. 'You've *got* to help me.'

Dr. Morelle frowned. 'I don't quite see how I could.'

'You can, believe me, or I wouldn't be phoning you. When I explain it, you'll see.'

'But when?'

'As soon as possible. Tonight.'

'This is preposterous!'

'Look, Dr. Morelle, I am talking from the garage; I usually close at ten o'clock. But I'll wait for you — you'll pass here on your way back to Conway,'

'This is most inconvenient . . . '

'I'll be here. Waiting for you, Dr. Morelle. I beg of you not to let me down!' With that urgent imprecation, Griffiths rang off.

Thoughtfully, Dr. Morelle replaced the receiver. 'And this was to be a quiet holiday,' he mused.

In the dining room, Evans finished his drink, and put down the glass. 'Thanks for the scotch, David, it really hit the spot.'

'You'll have a night-cap, Glyn?' Mary asked.

'Why, do I look as if I'm going to bed yet?'

Mary flushed slightly. 'No, of course not.'

Miss Frayle stood up. 'We must be getting along. It's been such a lovely evening.'

'Must you go?' Owen said genially. 'Ah, here's Dr. Morelle . . . '

'Was it anything important?' Miss Frayle asked anxiously. You haven't got to rush back to London tonight?'

'No, I'm glad to say.'

'So we'll see you and Miss Frayle at the rehearsal tomorrow night?' Evans queried.

'We're looking forward to it,' Miss Frayle assured him.

'Good.' Evans hesitated, then added: 'Come to think, perhaps I will get an early night.'

'I was just saying, Doctor, we should be going.'

Dr. Morelle nodded. 'Yes. Miss Frayle.'

'Pity you and Mary couldn't be there David,' Evans smiled. But you'll be otherwise engaged.'

'We shall be on the night-plane for Venice,' Mary said, 'if David hasn't forgotten the tickets.'

'Venice.' Miss Frayle sighed. 'How romantic. All those gondoliers singing love songs.'

'I think it's time for us to say goodnight, Professor,' Dr. Morelle said deliberately.

'And I must put in an hour's work in

the laboratory,' Evans said. 'If you'll excuse me . . . Goodnight, Miss Frayle.'

'I'll come with you,' Mary said. 'There are some notes you should have. I do hope you don't mind, Dr. Morelle?'

'Of course not, we must be going.'

Evans and Mary left together, and Owen glanced at Dr. Morelle.

'I suppose I shall get on with some work too. It's been nice seeing you, Dr. Morelle. By the way I'm sorry about Glyn Evans, I'm afraid he can be a bit of a bore.'

'I rather liked him,' Miss Frayle said.

Owen shook his head. 'I don't know that he ought to have inflicted his amateur theatricals on you.'

'I'm sure we are both quite looking forward to it, aren't we Dr. Morelle?'

'Quite, Miss Frayle.'

'I can tell you that your presence at their rehearsal will be something of an event for little Conway Amateur Dramatic Society,' Owen commented, as he saw them to the door.

★ ★ ★

Dr. Morelle was driving back to his holiday cottage at Conway, Miss Frayle in the front passenger seat. She glanced at him: 'So you're going to stop at the garage and see him, Dr. Morelle?'

'I said I would.'

'Here's the garage ahead,' Miss Frayle said unnecessarily, as it came into view. 'Looks closed up.'

'But Griffiths is awaiting. I'll stop the car here.'

As Griffiths came hurrying forward, Dr. Morelle wound down his side window.

'I'm glad to see you, Dr. Morelle. Hello Miss.'

'Hello.'

'Now what is it?' Dr. Morelle demanded. Griffiths glanced at Miss Frayle uncertainly.

'You can talk in front of me,' she assured him blithely. 'I know all the Doctor's secrets.' Then she added quietly, 'Well nearly all.'

'Okay, Miss. Listen, Doctor. Someone in this place is out to ruin me. Someone knows who I am, and they intend to blow the gaff.'

Doctor Morelle frowned. 'Haven't we

already been into this?'

'I don't mean you. I'm sorry for the way I talked earlier on,' Griffiths apologized. 'This is someone else. Simply because I was accused of a murder I never did. After two years I've built up my garage business and put the past behind me . . . '

'What evidence have you for all this?' Dr. Morelle asked sharply.

'It was tonight at the rehearsal of the show for the church funds. A dramatic sketch they're doing; sent in anonymously, they said.'

'We saw that you were in the local amateur dramatics — ' Miss Frayle began.

'Mr. Griffiths will tell us, Miss Frayle,' Dr. Morelle said irritably.

'Oh . . . '

'I was always keen on the stage,' Griffiths resumed. 'This sketch is a real blood-curdler. And d'you know what it's about? The strangling of a young girl.'

'You mean the plot resembles your own case?' Dr. Morelle asked.

'Word for word,' Griffiths assented. 'A replica of the scene between me and her that night.'

'How extraordinary,' Miss Frayle said.

Dr. Morelle shrugged. 'Dramatic plots are forever being devised by authors. It would not be unusual if one were imagined which would seem to fit your case.'

'This has certainly got it off pat. It's uncanny, the place, the time — the very hour.'

'Those details came out at the time of your trial,' Dr. Morelle pointed out. 'The author might have been present, or read the newspaper reports.'

Griffiths shook his head. 'I know it's someone who's found me out, and deliberately means to ruin me. So that I'll have to clear out.'

'With what object?' Dr. Morelle said shrewdly.

'I don't know,' Griffiths admitted miserably. 'But listen, Dr. Morelle there's something else I haven't told you about this play — I've been given the part of the murderer,'

'I see.'

'Come into the office, Dr. Morelle,' Griffiths invited, 'and you can read it for yourself.'

Dr. Morelle nodded. 'Very well. Out of the car, Miss Frayle.'

Griffiths opened the door to his small office. 'I'll switch the light on.'

As they waited behind him, Miss Frayle whispered to Dr. Morelle: 'How odd that Mr. Evans should have been talking about this — '

'What was that?' Griffiths turned.

'Nothing,' Miss Frayle said hastily.

Griffiths closed the office door behind them, then turned again. 'I thought you said something about Mr. Evans.'

'We met him this evening at Professor Owen's house,' Dr. Morelle said.

Griffiths nodded. 'I know, he's his assistant.'

'He had been at the rehearsal. That's all,' Miss Frayle added quickly.

'Yes, he's another who's stage-struck.' Griffiths crossed to his desk. 'Here you are, there's the little drama, Dr. Morelle.' He handed him some typewritten sheets, held together with a single staple at the top left corner.

'Thank you.' Dr. Morelle took the script, and glanced at the top sheet.

'Only a few pages to learn. But they're full of dynamite,' Griffiths said.

'What's it called?' Miss Frayle leaned to read the title. ' 'Act of Violence'. That's a gripping title, anyway.'

'It's gripping, and no mistake,' Griffiths said grimly. 'In every sense of the word. Just you read the last lines of the sketch, Dr. Morelle.'

'Shall I read it with you, Doctor?' Miss Frayle asked excitedly.

'Go on, Miss Frayle,' Griffiths invited, 'go ahead.'

'This is really rather fun, isn't it. Fancy I've never acted with you before, Doctor.'

Griffiths moved to the light switch near the door. 'I'll turn this light out — just leaving the desk-lamp on . . . Gives you the right atmosphere. You can see to read by.'

'It's quite dark and creepy,' Miss Frayle murmured.

'It isn't much of a part for the girl,' Griffiths said, coming back to the desk. 'As you'll see.'

'Oh, no love-scenes?' Miss Frayle pouted.

'Come along, Miss Frayle,' Dr. Morelle snapped impatiently. 'I'll begin here.'

He turned to a later sheet, holding it so that Miss Frayle could read alongside him.

'You haven't been quite so smart, up to date, my girl,' Dr. Morelle began.

'Why do you say that?'

'You've told me you live by yourself, that you haven't any relations and you won't be missed until you go back to work next week.'

'But why should I be missed then? You talk as if I'm not going back to work.' Miss Frayle's natural inflection of slight confusion fitted the words perfectly.

'Do I? How strange of me. Or am I being psychic?'

'What's the matter? Why are you staring at me in that funny way?'

'Turn your head away if you don't like to look at me.'

'But what is this? I don't like it. I'm frightened.' Miss Frayle voice took on a convincing tinge of simulated terror.

'Don't turn away, you'll see it all in the mirror.'

'What's that you're taking out of your pocket?'

'You can see in that mirror.'

'Oh, it's a pair of nylons — oh, the present you promised to give me.'

'You're mistaken, it's only one of a pair of nylons.'

'What's the use of one stocking?'

'It's the finest quality. See how soft it is.'

'Keep away.'

'Feel the texture — '

'No.'

' . . . around your throat — '

'Don't — ' Miss Frayle broke off with convincing choking sounds.

'That's it Doctor,' Griffiths said quietly. 'And that's how the real thing went, almost word for word.'

'Including your telling the girl to look in the mirror?' Dr. Morelle asked sharply.

'Yes,' Griffiths admitted. 'It's positively uncanny.'

Dr. Morelle looked thoughtful. 'It certainly is.'

'How very nasty.' Miss Frayle gave a little shudder.

217

'You can say that again. When I read it this evening, my blood ran cold,' Griffiths admitted.

'In actual fact,' Dr. Morelle said slowly 'what happened, as I remember you described it in the witness-box, was that you put the stocking round her neck to frighten her?'

'That's all I did, and then I left her.'

'And the real murderer came in afterwards?' Miss Frayle prompted.

'Yes, Miss, a few minutes afterwards, and strangled her with the stocking.'

'I always maintained that the real murderer was listening outside the door,' Dr. Morelle said slowly. 'He hid when you came out and then went in.'

'She certainly had plenty of men friends.' Griffiths shrugged. 'All sorts, young, middle-aged, rich and stupid. And the brainy sort.'

'What are you thinking, Dr. Morelle?' Miss Frayle asked. 'There's that look on your face.'

'Merely a notion that has occurred to me,' Dr. Morelle said briefly. 'Then we shall see you at tomorrow evening's rehearsal, Griffiths.'

'Are you going to be there?' Griffiths was surprised.

'We have already received an invitation.'

'We'll give you some moral support,' Miss Frayle added.

Griffiths tightened his lips. 'I'm going through with it, yes.'

Dr. Morelle nodded. 'I thought you would. To run away would simply provide your unseen adversary with the satisfaction of knowing he has scared you off.'

'And that's just his little game,' Griffiths muttered,

Dr. Morelle nodded. 'To stay and face the consequences might discourage any further attempt upon your peace of mind.'

'You're absolutely right, Doctor,' Griffiths declared. 'I'll show this anonymous so-and-so that Robert Griffiths doesn't scare so easily.'

★   ★   ★

Dr. Morelle was driving Miss Frayle back to their lodging. 'Take this next turning, Dr. Morelle, and we're almost home,' she said. 'It's been quite an evening, in a way. And I can hardly wait to see the rehearsal tomorrow.'

'It should provide a certain amount of interest, 'Dr. Morelle said dryly, deftly turning the wheel.

'All the same, it still baffles me that anyone could go to such lengths,' Miss Frayle admitted.

'The author of the sketch, not inappropriately titled 'Act of Violence', whoever he — or she — may be, has some motive which we may soon learn.'

Miss Frayle wrinkled her brow. 'It must have been someone locally, who'd not only found out about Griffiths, but calculated that he would have to re-enact his experiences.'

'That would appear to be a reasonable deduction,' Dr. Morelle agreed.

'But what for?'

'Man's darkest continent is the human mind, and its explorer encounters vast arid deserts of inhibition and secret fear,' Dr. Morelle said gravely.

'Yes, Doctor, but — ' Miss Frayle broke off as she was struck by a sudden thought. 'You said just now he — or she — You mean you think Miss Lloyd may have written it?'

★ ★ ★

Mary Lloyd was walking home along a country lane. Judging by her slow progress, she appeared to be extremely tired.

She halted as a cyclist overtook her, and braked in front of her. She recognized the rider at once.

'Sergeant Rees!'

'Hello, Miss Lloyd.' The young policeman dismounted, and turned back towards her, pushing his bike. 'What are you doing out at this time of night? Been to a party?'

Mary sighed. 'No, I haven't, I've just left the Professor.'

'Working late hours aren't you?'

Mary smiled. 'So are you.'

'I'm just back from the police-dance over at Conway. But I'll walk with you and see you home,' Rees offered.

'That is kind of you,' Mary resumed

her journey, the young policeman pushing his bike alongside. 'I was almost walking in my sleep,' she admitted.

Rees chuckled. 'You'll have to train Professor Owen better than this when you're Mrs. Owen.'

'Yes, I will,' Mary agreed sleepily.

'Little Conway is full of the wedding tomorrow,' Rees commented.

'How nice of them.'

'And to think your future husband's kept you working till past midnight,' Rees shook his head. 'What a slave-driver he is. He'll be wanting you to take the typewriter on your honeymoon.'

'I don't even know if there'll be one,' Mary laughed lightly. 'Well, here's my lodging . . . Just as well my landlady's used to me being back late.'

Rees looked at house they had reached, and nodded. 'She's heard us. I can see there's a light in the window.'

Mary smiled. 'Always likes to bolt up after me. Thank you so much Sergeant Rees . . . Goodnight,'

'A pleasure. And very best wishes for tomorrow. Good night, Miss Lloyd.'

★ ★ ★

'Oh, hello, Mr. Evans.'

'Good morning, Mrs. Parry.'

'Off for your early morning walk as per usual, sir?'

'Yes. I'll be out for about half-an-hour.'

'It's a lovely morning. And just right for the wedding. Real orange-blossom weather, you might say.'

'Yes, Mrs. Parry.'

Evans continued on his way along the country lane as the charwoman went on up the path to the front door of Professor Owen's house.

She let herself in with her own key, then closed the front door. She began humming the 'Wedding March' under her breath as she made her way to the kitchen.

'Better get the Professor's breakfast,' she murmured to herself. 'If you can call a cup of tea and a bit of toast breakfast.'

The hall clock began striking the half hour. 'Half-past-eight. I must get a move on . . . '

It was only a matter of minutes to prepare the frugal breakfast, then the

223

charwoman took it upstairs. 'Professor — I've brought your breakfast.' Balancing a tray in one hand, Mrs. Parry rapped lightly on Owen's bedroom door.

There was no response. 'Fast asleep,' she smiled. She knocked again, more loudly. 'I'd better go in,' she decided, and pushed open the door.

'Good morning, here's your breakfast, Professor. Come on now, wake up. It's your wedding day. Wake up, Professor — ' she broke off as she approached the bed.

Catching sight of the hideous expression on Owen's face, she gave a horrified gasp.

'*Oh — he's dead!*'

★ ★ ★

'Oh dear, the morning hasn't started before that thing goes!' Miss Frayle went to pick up the telephone as it rang stridently.

'Hello, this is Dr. Morelle's home at Conway.'

The agitated voice of Mary Lloyd crackled in the earpiece. 'I must speak to him. I must — '

'Who is that, please?'

'It's Mary Lloyd — is that Miss Frayle?'

'Yes, Miss Lloyd; is something wrong?'

'I must speak to Dr. Morelle. It's dreadfully urgent!'

'Will you hold on, please? Dr. Morelle's working, but I'll go and let him know.'

Miss Frayle opened the door to the room that was serving as Dr. Morelle's study. 'Dr. Morelle — '

'Ah, Miss Frayle, just take that Dictaphone cylinder, will you? Put it on the table.'

'But, Doctor — '

'Don't drop it. That's the worst of a makeshift study — no place for anything.'

'No, Doctor.'

'I fancy I am arriving somewhere in determining the difference between blood-groups in relation to the criminal tendencies of the person involved.'

Miss Frayle made another effort to engage his intention. 'Yes, I'm sure, but there's — '

'My belief,' Dr. Morelle resumed, 'that any emotional upheaval must give rise to certain glandular reactions, which in turn might have an effect upon the blood, undoubtedly has some basis.'

'Doctor, Miss Lloyd's on the phone,' Miss Frayle finally got her words out. Dr. Morelle resumed his lecture mode as if he had not heard her.

'And if this effect, apparent in the blood for a length of time afterwards, the conclusion to be drawn would — '

'She sounds in a frightful state,' Miss Frayle managed to interrupt.

'Who — ?'

'Mary Lloyd — who's marrying Professor Owen today — she's on the phone.'

'On the telephone? Why didn't you tell me?' Dr. Morelle admonished irritably. 'Standing there gossiping!'

'Yes, Dr. Morelle,' Miss Frayle said resignedly.

'I'll speak to her.' He got up and swept from the room, Miss Frayle trailing disconsolately in his wake.

'Miss Lloyd? Dr. Morelle here.' He listened intently to the distraught voice on the line.

'Something frightful's happened. Please

come at once, Doctor. Professor Owen's dead. He's been murdered!'

* * *

'It's such a lovely morning,' Miss Frayle said reflectively, as she and Dr. Morelle stood outside Professor Owen's home. Behind them, his car stood in the lane outside the gate.

'A wonderful view across the estuary,' Dr. Morelle murmured absently. 'Remarkably fine.'

The desultory conversation ceased as footsteps sounded inside the house, and the door opened.

'Good morning,' Miss Frayle said.

'Not very good for the poor Professor,' the charwoman said quietly.

'I'm Dr. Morelle . . . '

'Miss Lloyd's expecting us,' Miss Frayle added.

'Yes, come in.' Mrs. Parry stood back, then closed the door behind them as they entered. They looked at the dejected figure of the charwoman as she turned. She was clearly stunned.

Mrs. Parry spoke almost mechanically: 'I'd just arrived, and took him up his breakfast — not that he has much — '

'Where is Miss Lloyd?' Dr. Morelle interrupted gently.

'Upstairs in his bedroom — where I found him.'

'Come along. Miss Frayle,' Dr. Morelle snapped, moving to the stairs.

Mrs. Parry continued talking as Miss Frayle hesitated, looking at her sympathetically.

'I knocked and he didn't reply, I thought he was sleeping heavy, and then it being his wedding day and that, I went in . . . '

As the woman paused, Miss Frayle turned and hurried after Dr. Morelle. By the time she joined him inside the bedroom, he was already in conversation with Mary Lloyd.

'I telephoned you right away, Dr. Morelle. This is dreadful. The shock — '

'I'm so sorry, Miss Lloyd,' Miss Frayle commiserated, coming into the room.

Mary looked at Dr. Morelle anxiously. 'I didn't know what to do. Then I thought perhaps I ought to ask you to help.'

'This is how it was when you found him?' Dr. Morelle questioned sharply.

'Yes. I haven't touched anything.'

'A clear case of strangulation. I'm afraid there's nothing that can be done.'

'Poor thing,' Miss Frayle whispered.

'I should think death must have occurred several hours ago,' Dr. Morelle decided dispassionately, touching the dead man's skin to assess temperature. 'Are you all right, Miss Frayle?

'Yes, of course,' she said faintly.

'If you feel a trifle faint — '

'I know,' Miss Frayle said miserably. 'Just put my head between my knees.'

'I can't understand — who could have done this?' Mary glanced at her dead fiancé, then turned her head away quickly as Dr. Morelle addressed her again.

'You were with him late last night?'

Mary nodded miserably. 'There was a last batch of notes to be done, and he wanted to get it over with.'

'Where is Mr. Evans?' Dr. Morelle asked sharply.

'He'll be out on his morning walk, I'll ask Mrs. Parry if she's seen him.'

'Never mind that now,' Dr. Morelle advised.

Mary shrugged. 'He'll be back presently.'

'Doesn't he know about Professor Owen?' Miss Frayle asked.

'It would appear not,' Dr. Morelle murmured.

'There's no reason why he should. He always goes for a walk first thing, before starting work for the day,' Mary said.

'That explains it.' Dr. Morelle pointed, 'These test tubes over here — what are they doing in his bedroom?'

'They are to do with the work he was doing,' Mary explained. 'It was a kind of insecticide. A poisonous gas for killing insects of all kinds.'

'And he was experimenting here last night?' Dr. Morelle prompted.

'Oh, yes, you see — his bedroom's more like a workshop.'

'Would this gas kill people?' Miss Frayle asked, wide-eyed.

Mary nodded. 'That was what David

was working on, to make it non-fatal to human beings.'

'He was very absent-minded, wasn't he?' Miss Frayle said awkwardly.

'Never to do with his job,' Mary said firmly.

'When did you last see these test tubes?' Dr. Morelle questioned.

'In the laboratory, last night.'

'Can you explain their presence here?'

Mary thought for a moment. 'Perhaps he brought them up with him, to make a last-minute adjustment. How else could they have got up here?'

'There's no one in the house at night except Professor Owen and Mr. Evans?' Dr. Morelle continued his questioning.

'No.'

'Did the Professor invariably sleep with the windows closed?'

Mary nodded. 'Yes. As a matter of fact I came up here and put on the reading-lamp beside his bed. The insects started flying in from the dark, and I closed the window. When I left David was on his way up to bed.'

Miss Frayle looked towards the window

at the sound of footsteps on gravel. 'That sounds as if someone's outside in the drive.' She reached the window and looked down. 'It's Mr. Evans,'

Mary glanced at Dr. Morelle. 'Shall I tell him what's happened, Doctor?'

'Why not let him come up and see for himself?'

Mary shook her head. 'The shock — it might upset him.'

'You prefer to break the news to him?'

'It might be better. I'll catch him in case he meets Mrs. Parry. She'll be in the kitchen, but if she hears him — I'll hurry.'

As she went out, Dr. Morelle glanced irritably at Miss Frayle.

'Miss Frayle, when you've finished scrutinizing that dead moth on the window sill . . . '

'There's a whole lot of insects here,' Miss Frayle said wonderingly.

'Naturally, they died as a result of the poisonous gas with which Professor Owen was experimenting . . . Take off one of your stockings.'

'Yes, Doctor,' Miss Frayle said automatically, then raised her eyebrows, 'why, what do you mean?'

'Oh, don't be so coy. I want to test a theory.'

'Yes, Dr. Morelle,' Miss Frayle said meekly.

Dr. Morelle turned to look at the rigid body of Professor Owen. 'You have observed that the deceased had been strangled with a silk stocking?'

'Oh, no, I — I hadn't looked properly. It's not very nice.' Miss Frayle fumbled with one of her stockings.

'Murder hardly ever is,' Dr. Morelle said dryly, turning.

'There you are, Doctor.' Miss Frayle passed him one of her stockings. 'It's my best pair. Try not to ladder it — ' she gave a little gasp. 'Oh!'

Dr. Morelle frowned. 'What Miss Frayle?'

'Nylon stockings. The man at the garage. Griffiths. That girl was strangled with a nylon stocking!'

'You perceive some connection?' Dr. Morelle asked dryly.

'You mean — ? But — ?'

'Perhaps a demonstration will help clear the fog that seems to be obscuring your mind,' Dr. Morelle said patiently. 'Come here.'

'Yes, Doctor.'

'Give me the stocking.' Wonderingly, Miss Frayle placed it in his hand. 'Thank you. Now, I am moving towards you as if — ' Miss Frayle's eyes widened, ' — as if about to attack you.'

'Oh — '

'Now, grip me with your right hand,' Dr. Morelle instructed.

'Like this?' Miss Frayle reached out.

'Your *right* hand!' Dr. Mortelle snapped. 'As if to ward me off.'

'Oh, yes — you've got me quite flustered . . . But, Doctor, I never would — Like this?'

'Do it as if you mean it, as if you know I'm about to murder you,' Dr. Morelle sighed, 'which as a matter of fact — '

'What, Doctor?'

'Never mind, never mind.'

'Is this right?' Miss Frayle shot out her right hand and fastened it around the front of Dr. Morelle's throat.

'You are not supposed to strangle me!' Dr. Morelle choked.

'Sorry!'

'Now, do you see how I'm holding the stocking?' Dr. Morelle said heavily.

Realization dawned. 'You mean, you haven't knotted it — just twisted it round my neck?'

'Precisely. Now, the stocking round his neck has been *tied in a knot* . . . As a close look will show you.'

'I'll take your word for it, Doctor,' Miss Frayle said hastily. 'Which indicates — what?'

'That you might telephone for the police, Miss Frayle.'

Miss Frayle glanced about her. 'Oh, there's a phone over there — ' she broke off, and looked at Dr. Morelle. 'Shall I use a handkerchief to hold the receiver?'

Dr. Morelle smiled condescendingly. 'If it amuses you to do so.'

'I meant in case there're fingerprints —' Miss Frayle began.

'If there are, they won't prove anything one way or the other. And wrapping a handkerchief round the receiver will only serve to smudge them.'

'But I always thought — '

'Your head is forever plagued with peculiar fallacies, Miss Frayle,' Dr. Morelle snapped. 'Just pick up the phone and get the police!'

'Yes, Dr. Morelle,' Miss Frayle gulped. Then, glancing out of the window: 'Oh, there's Miss Lloyd and Mr. Evans in the garden.'

'So I observed.'

'I suppose she's telling him about poor Professor Owen,' Miss Frayle remarked.

'No doubt she is doing that,' Dr. Morelle agreed dryly.

Outside, in the front garden below, Glyn Evans was conversing with Mary.

'Mary, I can't believe this has happened — '

'I don't know what to believe,' she said miserably.

'You must keep a grip on yourself,' Evans told her. 'Dr. Morelle's up there, is he?'

'Yes, I phoned him at once.' Mary looked at Evans appealingly. 'I couldn't think what else to do. I arrived a few minutes after Mrs. Parry and you'd gone out.'

'I don't see what this has got to do with him,' Evans remarked, tightening his lips.

Mary looked surprised. 'He's a doctor.'

'I'd better see what's going on,' Evans decided, and moved towards the house, Mary following him.

Evans glanced at her: 'Please believe I'll do everything I can to help you,' he said earnestly.

In the bedroom upstairs, Miss Frayle had continued to linger at the window. 'They're still talking there, Doctor. It must be a bit of a shock for Mr. Evans too. Doctor — ?' She glanced round. 'Oh, he's gone,' she told herself. 'And I'd better phone the police.'

As Evans and Mary came into the house they saw Dr. Morelle descending the stairs into the hall.

'Oh, there you are, Dr. Morelle,' Evans said. 'Mary and I were just coming up to you.'

Dr. Morelle reached the foot of the stairs and held up a hand. 'I think it better if no one goes into the bedroom until the police get here.'

'Police?' Mary said nervously.

'Naturally. They are being sent for.'

'Mary says he's been strangled,' Evans said slowly. 'Murder.'

'It would appear to be the case.' Dr. Morelle gave Evans a sharp look. 'You worked very closely with him, did you not?'

Evans nodded promptly. 'Yes, we were experimenting with a form of gas to exterminate agricultural pests, rodents, and so forth. David and I developed it so that it could be a workable proposition.'

'Maybe we should move into the lounge?' Mary suggested.

Dr. Morelle nodded, and the two men followed her into the room. They found seats around the table near the bay windows.

Dr. Morelle looked at Evans and resumed his questioning. 'And after you finished your work last night, did you see him again?'

'No, I went straight to bed.' Evans shrugged. 'I was pretty tired, as you will remember. After all that rehearsing.'

Mary looked towards the doorway. 'Here's Miss Frayle.'

Miss Frayle entered the room and looked at Dr. Morelle who gave her a questioning glance. 'I've spoken to the local police station,' she reported. 'The sergeant is on his way.'

'Sergeant Rees — I saw him late last night,' Mary said.

'Did you, Miss Lloyd?' Dr. Morelle asked sharply.

'Yes, he was on his bike. He walked home with me.'

'What time was this?'

Mary reflected. 'It was about twelve o'clock.'

'I see . . . ' Dr. Morelle looked thoughtful. Before he could speak again the doorbell rang.

Evans half rose. 'That'll probably be him.'

Mary waved her hand. 'Mrs. Parry will let him in.' Evans sat down again.

Dr. Morelle rose to his feet. 'I will return to Professor Owen's room. Everyone please remain here.'

'Won't you need me, Doctor?' Miss Frayle asked.

Dr. Morelle smiled sardonically. 'I

think we shall be able to manage without you, Miss Frayle.'

Dr. Morelle went out into the hall, and saw that Mrs. Parry had admitted the police sergeant. He introduced himself, then accompanied Rees up to Professor Owen's bedroom.

Rees straightened up from examining the dead man. 'It looks like a serious business, Dr. Morelle. How long would you say he's been dead?'

'Death must have ensued somewhere between midnight and the early hours of this morning.'

'Miss Lloyd had left him just about twelve o'clock,' Rees said. 'I met her on the way home.'

Dr. Morelle nodded. 'She mentioned that fact to me. There was no reference to any quarrel between them?'

Rees shook his head emphatically. 'Good heavens, no. They were getting married today.' He looked at Dr. Morelle: 'You don't think that Miss Lloyd — ?'

'Someone did, Sergeant.'

'I can't believe it. Yet,' Rees mused, 'it was a woman's silk stocking — what are you looking at, Dr. Morelle?'

'These insects on the window-ledge here.' Dr. Morelle indicated them.

'They're all dead,' Rees said slowly.

'Supposing,' Dr. Morelle suggested, 'Professor Owen had noticed them and thought they provided a good opportunity to experiment with them?'

'With that poison gas stuff?'

Dr. Morelle nodded. 'Which proved efficacious — not only on the insects, but on himself as well.'

'It wasn't quite safe for human beings to use,' Rees mused. 'I remember Miss Lloyd telling me about it, once. And Mr. Evans — he's spoken about it to me.'

'Quite.'

'And someone else got at it, you mean?' Rees went on. 'And tried to make it look as if he'd been strangled?'

'Now perceive the significance of these dead insects,' Dr. Morelle said enigmatically.

The police sergeant frowned, 'How do they help?'

'They were attracted by the reading-lamp and shut in when Miss Lloyd closed the window. Her alibi would appear indisputable.'

'I certainly know where she was about midnight,' Rees said.

'But we have only her word that the Professor was in fact alive when she left him,' Dr. Morelle pointed out. 'Except for the fact that the insects when the poisonous gas killed them, at the same time as Professor Owen, were at the window. Why?'

Rees frowned. 'Search me.'

'Because,' Dr. Morelle explained, 'they were *attracted there by the first light of daybreak*.'

The sergeant's frown gave way to a smile. 'You're right, Dr. Morelle!'

'Naturally, Sergeant Rees,' Dr. Morelle smiled complacently.

'Whoever caused his death did it at daybreak,' Rees said excitedly..

'Daylight is beginning to break for you, also,' Dr. Morelle commented dryly.

'So it couldn't have been Miss Lloyd.' Rees frowned again. 'Then who?'

'Are you interested in amateur theatricals, Sergeant?' Dr. Morelle asked,

Rees looked surprised. 'Not specially, no; why?'

'It is a form of relaxation for some. Today is going to be busy for you, but why not join me at a rehearsal this evening of the little Conway Dramatic Society?'

Rees gave a blank look. 'I don't see what it could have to do with this business.'

'I don't think you will be wasting your time,' Dr. Morelle said quietly.

'Well, I — that is, I mean — '

Dr. Morelle smiled sardonically. 'Unless, of course, you will have already decided upon the culprit.'

★　★　★

Miss Frayle was seated alongside Dr. Morelle as he drove his car in the direction of Little Conway. She glanced at her watch.

'It's five-thirty, Dr. Morelle; we're due there at six o'clock, aren't we?'

'I want to arrive a few minutes before,' Dr. Morelle explained patiently, 'to have a word with Sergeant Rees.'

'I really can't wait to see this rehearsal,' Miss Frayle enthused.

'One or two others will be interested, I imagine,' Dr. Morelle murmured.

'Robert Griffiths for one,' Miss Frayle agreed. She glanced at Dr. Morelle curiously. 'What were you talking to him over the phone about this afternoon?'

Dr. Morelle kept his eye on the road. He spoke casually: 'Just an idea I had which I thought might be helpful for this evening's performance.'

Miss Frayle settled back in her seat. 'You sound very enigmatic . . . I'm surprised that Mr. Evans will be there.'

'He seemed to feel that despite the tragedy, nothing could be gained by not attending the rehearsal,' Dr. Morelle murmured.

Miss Frayle again showed her fondness for cliché. 'The show-must-go-on idea?'

'That sort of sentiment, no doubt.'

Miss Frayle pursed her lips. 'Poor Miss Lloyd. It's been terrible for her.'

'Most distressing,' Dr. Morelle agreed, deftly taking a turning into the village.

'I never thought she'd collapse the way she did, though,' Miss Frayle went on thoughtfully.

'A case of delayed reaction. She will recover after sedatives and complete rest.'

Miss Frayle sighed. 'She must have been very much in love with Professor Owen.'

'So it would seem.'

'There's the village-hall, just ahead,' Miss Frayle said unnecessarily, as the building came into clear view. 'We're in plenty of time.'

'Sergeant Rees is there, awaiting us,' Dr. Morelle stated.

Miss Frayle looked ahead myopically, then nodded. 'Oh, yes. And is that a police-car there, that black one next to the sports car?'

'Possibly.'

Dr. Morelle slowed his car and brought it to a stop. Sergeant Rees, who had been watching out for them, approached their car quickly.

Dr. Morelle got out and opened the door for Miss Frayle as Rees came up.

'Hello, Dr. Morelle . . . Miss Frayle.'

'Good evening,' Dr. Morelle murmured.

'Hello, Sergeant Rees,' Miss Frayle said brightly. 'Any news?'

The police sergeant shook his head. 'Nothing since this morning. Caenarvon C.I.D. have taken over. Two of them are here.' He nodded towards the black car parked nearby.

'Have all the dramatic society people arrived?' Dr. Morelle asked.

'The one we want has, anyway,' Rees answered enigmatically. 'Rehearsal's just beginning.'

'Then we'll go on in,' Dr. Morelle murmured.

The rehearsals for the concert proceeded, with various acts and recitals until the time came for the play 'Act of Violence' to be enacted. Robert Griffiths and a young and pretty actress took their places on the stage, both holding typescripts of the sketch.

Dr. Morelle was seated at the beginning of an aisle, with Miss Frayle between himself and Sergeant Owen. They began to watch and listen more closely. Miss Frayle tensed as the climax of the play was reached.

Griffiths was speaking the man's role: 'You haven't been quite so smart up to date, my girl.'

'Why do you say that?'

'You've told me you lived by yourself, that you haven't any relatives and you won't be missed until you go back to work next week.'

Miss Frayle whispered: 'I think you acted the part just as well as he's doing, Dr. Morelle.'

'*Quiet!*' Dr. Morelle whispered fiercely.

'But why should I be missed then?' the girl said, puzzled. 'You talk as if I'm not going back to work.'

'Do I? How strange of me. Or am I being psychic?'

'What's the matter?' the girl faltered. 'Why are you staring at me in that funny way?'

'And I was as good as her!' Miss Frayle muttered, *sotto voce*.

'You don't have to look at me,' Griffiths read.

'Something's different, Doctor!' Miss Frayle gripped his arm.

'*Shush!*' he snapped.

'There's no mirror!' Miss Frayle whispered.

The girl's voice rose: 'But what is this? I don't like it, I'm frightened.'

'Don't turn away.'

'What's that you're taking out of your pocket?'

'You can see for yourself.'

'Oh, it's a pair of nylons — oh, the present you promised to give me.'

'What's the use of one stocking?' the girl said wonderingly.

'It's the finest quality,' Griffiths murmured. 'See how soft it is.'

'Keep away.'

'Feel the texture — '

'No,'

' . . . around your throat!'

'Don't — *oooh!*

The girl's choking sounds became mixed with a couple of handclaps from some of their fellow players as the curtain fell.

Miss Frayle turned to Sergeant Rees. 'What did you think of it, Sergeant Rees?'

'Very dramatic. I'm sure everyone will be hanging on to their seats on Monday night.'

'But it's been changed,' Miss Frayle said, frowning. 'The ending was a bit different — ' she broke off as Dr. Morelle suddenly got to his feet on the end of the aisle. 'Dr. Morelle — where are you going?'

'Excuse me, Miss Frayle!' To her astonishment, Sergeant Rees was also on his feet, and roughly pushed past her to join Dr. Morelle in the aisle.

'Come on, Sergeant Rees,' Dr. Morelle urged.

'He'll be at the back of the stage,' Rees said.

'Who?' Miss Frayle blinked. 'Mr. Griffiths?'

Neither man answered her, both hurrying up onto the stage and vanishing through the curtains.

'You might wait for me!' Miss Frayle called after them.

As Dr. Morelle and Sergeant Rees passed through the curtain the first person they encountered was the girl actress.

'Are you looking for someone?'

'Mr. Evans,' Dr. Morelle said briefly.

'Oh, behind the scenery on the other

side of the stage.'

'Thank you,' Dr. Morelle said, 'and may I congratulate you on your performance.'

'Oh, how kind — ' the girl began, then broke off in surprise as both men turned and rushed across the stage to where Evans was emerging from some scenery.

'Oh — Dr. Morelle. Hello, Sergeant Rees,' Evans muttered as he caught sight of them.

'May I offer my congratulations to you,' Dr. Morelle spoke without warmth. 'But you appear somewhat agitated . . . ?'

A strange look crossed Evans's face. 'Of course I am!' he snapped. 'The whole thing was ruined!'

'Indeed?' Dr. Morelle prompted gently.

'The mirror!' Evans's voice rose. 'There was no mirror. He should have strangled her while she was looking at him in the mirror. *And it wasn't there!*'

'Was its presence so important?' Dr. Morelle asked.

'Important!' Evans's voice shook with anger and frustration. 'Don't you understand, that's what really happened! *That's why I wrote the sketch.* That's why . . . '

He broke off, staring into the set faces of Dr. Morelle and Rees. 'What have I said?' he whispered.

'Nothing that surprises me. Mr. Evans,' Dr. Morelle said grimly.

'You mean . . . you knew?' Evans seemed to deflate. 'You knew all along?'

'It was evident that the anonymous author was someone living locally,' Dr. Morelle said incisively. 'I had already reached the conclusion that he felt an obsessive urge to confess some deadly secret. From my own inside knowledge, it became obvious to me moreover that the author was himself the murderer of that girl! The position of the mirror — that was something which no one but the murderer could have known.'

Evans clutched at his throat. 'I — I must get some air — can't breathe . . . '

'It was to be your fate to come to live here to encounter the very man who might have hanged for your crime,' Dr. Morelle said implacably.

Evans looked about him wildly. 'I must open the door.'

251

'You are the anonymous author of the dramatic sketch based on the Robert Griffiths case,' Dr. Morelle went on relentlessly, 'and you also murdered Professor Owen!'

'He took Mary from me,' Evans's voice was anguished, 'I was the one she really loved — '

'You knew about Griffiths — that he'd been convicted of strangling that girl you killed, and had been reprieved — and you knew that the sketch you'd written would be bound to plant suspicion on him for Owen's murder if a silk stocking was involved.'

'You can't prove it — ' Evans looked wildly about him.

'You added a lethal dose to the poisonous gas,' Dr. Morelle stated accusingly.

'I wasn't going to let him marry her!' Evans snarled.

Dr. Morelle nodded. 'You'd see him dead first. You made it look as if he'd been strangled by a nylon stocking.'

'I — I — My head's spinning,' Evans staggered. 'I must get some air.'

Rees stepped forward. 'I'll have to ask

you to come with me — '

Miss Frayle walked on to the stage from the wings. 'There you are, Dr. Morelle. I've just seen Robert Griffiths, and he says you asked him to take the mirror out of the script — '

'Yes, yes, Miss Frayle — ' Dr. Morelle said, irritated at the interruption.

'You can't prove anything anyway — I can't breathe — let me get some air — ' Evans suddenly made a bolt for it. He brushed past Miss Frayle, spinning her round so that she stumbled forward and collided with Sergeant Rees as he tried to follow.

'Come back — Mr. Evans — come back!' Rees shouted.

Ignoring the dazed Miss Frayle, Dr. Morelle grabbed Rees by the hand and dragged him upright. The two men then followed the fleeing figure along a corridor.

Ahead of them, Evans had reached a fire door. He thrust at the bars, bursting the door open, and vanished outside.

'Come back — stop him — stop him!' Rees shouted.

As they followed the fugitive outside,

they heard the sound of a car starting up.

'Damnation!' Rees panted, breathing hard. 'He's made a run for it!' He glanced at Dr. Morelle. 'Excuse me, Doctor!' He went across to the black police vehicle in the car park.

'I don't think he'll get far,' Dr. Morelle murmured after him.

Robert Griffiths came up. 'Ah, there you are, Dr. Morelle. Well, what did you think of it?'

Dr. Morelle gave him a thin smile. 'Most satisfactory. You followed my instructions to the letter.'

Griffiths frowned. 'Was that Evans who went out?' He caught sight of his speeding vehicle. 'That's his sports car!'

'He was in need of a little air,' Dr. Morelle said dryly.

'What the devil . . . we've got more rehearsing to do,' Griffiths said.

Dr. Morelle shook his head. 'You needn't trouble yourself about 'Act of Violence'. It was a case of one performance only.'

'He's driving at a hell of a lick,' Griffiths commented. 'What's come over him? He's stepping on — ' he broke off as there came the wail of a police siren from a black car in pursuit.

As both men stood watching the chase Miss Frayle came up behind them.

'Doctor? Hello, Mr. Griffiths. Where's Sergeant Rees? And — oh!' she broke off as the air was split by the sound of a crashing car.

'What was that?' Miss Frayle stammered, shaken.

Griffiths glanced round at her. 'It's Evans . . . He's smashed his car.'

Miss Frayle came alongside the two men and followed their gaze up the road.

There was a sudden flash and explosion ahead of the black police car

'His car . . . it's caught fire!' Miss Frayle gasped. 'You can see the flames!'

'You saw the crazy way he drove that car, Doctor,' Griffiths said.

'Yes.'

Griffiths gave him a sharp glance. 'You think he did it purposefully?'

Dr. Morelle nodded calmly. 'He did. You see, Evans was not only the killer of Professor Owen — he was also the original killer of the girl whose murder you were accused of! And he knew I could prove it.'

Miss Frayle was amazed. 'But, Dr. Morelle, how could you possibly have discovered that?'

'I knew as soon as I read the script that the anonymous author of the script was almost certainly the real murderer.' Dr. Morelle looked at Griffiths. 'You see, there was no mention at your trial that you had commanded the girl to look in the mirror while you were supposed to be strangling her. Nor was it in any of the newspaper reports. Details about the nylon stocking, yes — but *not* the mirror. The only two living people who knew you had used those words were yourself and the real murderer, who had overheard you from his concealment!'

Griffiths nodded dazedly. 'That's right! Hell, I should have realized . . . Damned smart deduction, Doctor!'

Miss Frayle exclaimed: 'Doctor Morelle always notices things the rest of us miss!'

'Thank you, Miss Frayle,' Dr. Morelle smiled faintly. Then noticing her puzzled expression, he added: 'Is something still troubling you?'

Yes, Doctor, I still don't see how the murder of Professor Owen was connected — '

'Evans had fallen in love with Miss Lloyd — he admitted it just now when I confronted him.' Dr. Morelle gave his superior smile. 'When she announced that she was going to marry Owen — a much older man — Evans's ego couldn't accept it. His murderous nature reasserted itself. He wanted Mary Lloyd for himself. He had already written the play about the earlier murder, and realized that he could use it to throw suspicion on Griffiths for the death of Owen!'

There was a pause as Miss Frayle grappled to assimilate what she had heard.

'I see . . . I think. But how could anyone be so horrible, Doctor?'

Dr. Morelle shrugged. 'The twisted mind seeks to achieve its purpose by twisted means.'

THE END

DR. MORELLE MEETS MURDER
A CASE FOR DR. MORELLE
DR. MORELLE'S CASEBOOK

We do hope that you have enjoyed reading this large print book.

Did you know that all of our titles are available for purchase?

We publish a wide range of high quality large print books including:
Romances, Mysteries, Classics
General Fiction
Non Fiction and Westerns

Special interest titles available in large print are:
The Little Oxford Dictionary
Music Book, Song Book
Hymn Book, Service Book

Also available from us courtesy of Oxford University Press:
Young Readers' Dictionary
(large print edition)
Young Readers' Thesaurus
(large print edition)

For further information or a free brochure, please contact us at:
Ulverscroft Large Print Books Ltd.,
The Green, Bradgate Road, Anstey,
Leicester, LE7 7FU, England.
Tel: (00 44) **0116 236 4325**
Fax: (00 44) **0116 234 0205**

MAKE IT NYLONS

Gordon Landsborough

Joe P. Heggy, professional trouble-buster for an international construction firm, is travelling to Turkey. As the plane lands in Istanbul he looks out of the window and witnesses a murder — a man being stabbed. The victim was the leader of the country's Ultra-Nationalist Party. That glimpse of murder brings him trouble. Millions of fanatics try to pin the crime on him — his life is in danger. His only ally — an Amazonian Rumanian peasant with a passion for western nylons!

THE PREDATORS

Sydney J. Bounds

Following years of hard training, Lee Sabre graduates as a Predator, First Class — an instrument of the Galactic Federation, which has conquered and subjugated his homeworld of Terra — once known as the Earth. The Federation sends Sabre and his team on their first space mission, where he is approached by the Terran Underground, an organisation determined to overthrow their alien yoke . . . and his decision could have a devastating effect on millions of lives, and the existence of Earth itself.

THE LAS VEGAS AFFAIR

Norman Lazenby

Johnny Lebaron arrives in Las Vegas, leaving behind an unhappy marriage in New York. His hopes of a quiet vacation are dashed when he meets the beautiful Dulie Grande. Only recently out of jail, she seeks vengeance on the man who put her there — crooked casino owner Nat Franz. Johnny and Dulie, caught up in her vendetta against Franz, must fight for their lives against organised crime and a psychotic hit man with orders to kill them . . .

FERAL

Steve Hayes & David Whitehead

There's something not quite right about Shelby's Oasis, the tourist trap in the middle of the Arizona desert. The Shelby sisters, Agnes and Diana, have more skeletons than closets in which to hide them. And with rumours of a fortune in gold buried on the property, who can be trusted — the sisters' scheming brother Scott? The seductive Kelly-Anne? Or Mitch, the loner who stumbles into their lives? One thing's for sure: nothing at Shelby's Oasis is what it seems . . .

THE RED INSECTS

John Russell Fearn

Nick Hansley, his wife Ena and father-in-law find that their country house, The Cedars, radiates a positively evil aura. Their strange neighbour Dr. Lexton calls, wanting to buy their home. But who is Dr. Lexton? And as for Ena's deceased uncle, entomologist Cyrus Odder, what was the nature of the secret experiment he had worked on there? Then after a mysterious death in the house — death spreads its net across the countryside — and the entire world . . .